The second book in the Calvin Arthur series

I0626183

In Calvin Arthur's

5th Grade Shoes

Quest for Courage

R. A. Stone

US Copyright Office

Stone, R. A.

5th Grade Shoes ~ *Quest for Courage*

Copyright © 2023

Editors: Rob Stone, Sarah Odren, Lamar and Anita Ekbladh

Printed in the United States
        10 9 8 7 6 5 4 3 2 1

Dedication

To all of my past students from Evan G. Shortlidge Elementary, David W. Harlan Intermediate, Avon Grove Elementary and Intermediate, Skyline Middle, and William F. Cooke Elementary. Our time together was short, but our countless interactions were all very inspirational and meaningful to me. Thanks for the memories.

With special thanks to my wife Kristin and our children Eric and Annika. I love you to planet "Pi" and back!

Introduction

It's the 1977-1978 school year and Calvin Arthur is on his way to fifth grade. When he arrives, he quickly finds out that he has been assigned to a teacher he really needs. Mrs. Walton is a star within her classroom. She is also the judge and jury that solve many problems swiftly. Calvin is intimidated by his new teacher and also finds himself in the middle of some classmate problems. Is this going to be a year of misery or does Calvin find courage along with some great experiences? Much like his fourth-grade year, he will surely be riding on an emotional roller coaster. See and feel what issues Calvin faces and you will relate to some of his pain and victories. Does this resemble your fifth-grade year? If you are reading this second book in the series, consider yourself a Calvin Arthur fan and please leave an Amazon review. It will help keep Calvin's message alive. You may contact R.A. Stone for school assembly information at fairway36@yahoo.com.

Table of Contents

1. The Famous Mrs. Walton   11
2. Safety Patrol   17
3. Jealousy   23
4. Snitch   27
5. Unshowy   33
6. The Cigarette   37
7. Nosebleed   41
8. The Target Is on Me   45
9. The Talk   51
10. Balderdash!   59
11. Bathroom in the Classroom   63
12. Mary Heelman   73
13. Willy Robot   79
14. Dirty Sock   83
15. Science Olympics   91
16. The Kickball Challenge   107
17. Epic Sleepover (part 1)   113
18. Epic Sleepover (part 2)   129
19. The End or Beginning   145
Final Comment   151
About the Author/Special Note   153

There is a question that is asked on only one night of the year. Some kids might love it, while some might dread it. Dinner at the Arthur house was always full of questions. Tonight, was no different.

Mom asked, "So Calvin, do you know what you are going to wear tomorrow for your first day of fifth grade?"

That was the dreaded question that I knew was coming. Those words meant that summer vacation was officially over. A funny feeling settled into the pit of my stomach as I said, "I wish summer wouldn't end. It went so quick. I guess I'll wear my jeans and a collar shirt from last year."

Mom said, "Why wouldn't you wear one of your new shirts?"

I answered with, "I just don't want to stand out too much on the first day. I don't want to seem too flashy. Blending in with my old clothes is okay by me, but I will be wearing my new high-top sneakers."

The next morning brought on more nervousness than I expected. The butterflies in my belly seemed to be growing with every bite of cereal. I was the only one left at the breakfast table as my two sisters, Candice and Clare, had just ventured out to their bus stop. They were off to a new year at middle school. I always wondered what it would be like to ride a bus to school. The walk to Washington Elementary was just under a mile. That distance meant no bus riding for me. I would be walking again this year.

After I walked about three city blocks this morning, I heard someone call out, "Hey Calvin, what's up?" I looked up and across the street I saw my buddy James Hopper from the other side of Wellington Heights.

I yelled back, "I'm on my way to fifth grade, James, what's up with you?"

"Obviously, I'm doing the same thing. Who is your teacher?" James asked.

As the light changed, I crossed in the crosswalk and approached James. "I have Mrs. Walton. What about you?"

Before James answered he said, "Ah man good luck to you, she is the mean one! I have Ms. Joseph, the nice one."

We began to walk together now and continued our discussion. "There were only two fifth grade classrooms James. I wonder how they decide which teacher we all get?"

"Not sure, but you will be okay in the strict class. Just roll with it, buddy," replied James with a not so reassuring tone in his voice.

"Easy for you to say, James. I'm even more nervous now."

We walked the rest of the way to school and talked about what we looked forward to this year.

"So, James what do you hope for in fifth grade?" I asked.

"I'm hoping to become a leader in my class and possibly in the school. What about you Calvin?"

"I'm looking forward to standing up for myself when Ashley, Vinney, Eddie or anyone else tries to bully me or push my buttons. I'm also going to help others who are getting bullied. You know, stand up for what is right."

"Wow, that's admirable. Have you been working out?" James asked.

"As a matter of fact, I have, and I'm feeling good. A summer of swim team, lifting weights, and growing three inches will change a guy." I responded.

James asked. "So, are you some kind of super hero now?"

"Well, how about we go with a concerned classmate with courage. I just want to make a difference this year."

With the sound of skepticism in his voice, James replied, "Oh well you do look a little taller."

We made it to Bishop Boulevard and crossed the busy intersection with the crossing guard's help. Then it was a straight walk to the front steps of Washington Elementary. The butterflies were now flapping in my belly. I had to take a deep breath to settle them down. My mind wondered and my head spun with the sight of kids everywhere. *Maybe, I didn't have as much courage as I thought? Maybe I'm not ready to make a difference?*

Upon entering the school, we knew just where to go. James and I walked all the way down to the end of the older kid's hall to the last two classrooms. I started to turn left and James went right. James looked back, smiled and said, "Have fun Calvin, see you at recess." Just before I went inside Mrs. Walton's classroom, I couldn't help notice that a lot of noise was coming from Ms. Joseph's class and that there was not a sound coming from my new class. Oh, how I wished that I could go right.

To my surprise, my new class had about fourteen students already sitting down and nobody was talking. In a quite boisterous voice, Mrs. Walton said, "Welcome Calvin Arthur. Your seat is over here."

I thought, *how could she know my name already*? Mrs. Walton continued talking to everyone about the plays she was in, or was a part of, over the summer at the Shea Theater. She was passionate about her plays and each student seemed to be focused on every word that she spoke. She was very dramatic and interesting. It was as if she was an amazing actress who was now our teacher. She was dressed in a bright colored floral dress with yellow high heels and matching yellow dangling earrings. One could tell she was no nonsense, intense, a bit intimidating, and that she loved her place in the classroom. It was as if her room was her stage, and she was the star performer.

As I looked around, I saw a variety of students. There were several kids from the Vineyard Apartments, Southern Pines and Rockville neighborhoods. Someone must have put us in that room for a reason. Mrs. Walton wasn't as mean as James said she would be. She was firm, organized, interesting, and attractive all at the same time. I wondered, *would she squash my desire for courage or embrace it? I guess time will tell.* She seemed to be everything you could ask for in a fifth grade teacher.

Mrs. Walton asked for a show of hands for who was interested in being a Safety Patrol member. As I looked around, I saw almost everyone's hand go up. With all of those hands, I didn't bother raising mine as I knew I wouldn't get picked. I guess my show of bravery will have to wait. Mrs. Walton said, "Oh my, I can't possibly pick all of you, so we need to come up with a way to make the selection process fair."

Someone yelled out, "Just put our names in a hat and select how many you need." Mrs. Walton did not respond to calling out so that idea was probably not going to be an option.

Ashley Anderson had her hand up and Mrs. Walton said, "What do you think Ashley?" She said, "We should write an essay on why we deserve to be chosen." You could hear a pin drop as we waited for Mrs. Walton to respond.

"Capital idea," she yelled out loud. Mrs. Walton had a way of capturing everyone's attention by projecting her voice a few octaves higher whenever necessary. She also kept filling up our brains with new words that made us think.

Mrs. Walton handed the newly assigned paper passer, Chucky McManus, a stack of five-line writing paper and told him to give one to everyone.

Jesse Salvador spoke up and asked, "Mrs. Walton, if we don't want to be on Safety Patrol, do we have to write?" Mrs. Walton did not respond to Jesse directly due to him not raising his hand, but she began giving the class information on how to write a persuasive essay.

At the end of her lecture she added, "Those of you who do not want to be on Safety Patrol should write about how you would like the Safety Patrol person to be. This will help in the selection process. Remember we can have eight students from each fifth grade class on the patrol."

I wrote that I thought a Safety Patrol member should be able to follow rules, not fool around, and understand their power limits. I remember being yelled at by a Safety last year for walking down the middle of the hallway at dismissal time. He made me go back where I came from, and told me to walk on the right side. I definitely thought that was an abuse of power.

The very next day, during writing time, our papers were being passed back. Chucky threw Ashley's paper with the word "Excellent" written on top at her feet on the ground. I couldn't tell if he was still mad that Ashley's idea made us all write papers, or jealous that she had the word "Excellent" written on top. As I watched him pass out more papers, I noticed he threw a few others on the floor near students. Each paper had the word "Excellent" written on top. At this point, I had what Chucky was doing figured out, and so did Mrs. Walton. She yelled out in a really deep and scary voice, "Chucky McManus!" Followed by a surprisingly calm voice, "You and I will spend some quality recess time together." Scared silence fell over the room.

My paper had the word "Good" on the top, but also had an additional note that said, "See me." *Oh my,* I thought, *why does she want to see me?* I also am not sure when I should see her. I am somewhat shy when dealing with adults, so this issue started to weigh on me. I decided I would go up to her when we return from recess. It's all I could think about. I felt nervous to speak one on one with Mrs. Walton.

Recess was uneventful as I decided to climb on the monkey bars and go down the slide a bit. I just didn't feel like playing kickball today. As soon as we went inside, I went straight up to Mrs. Walton and asked, "Is this a good time to see you?"

Mrs. Walton replied, "Yes, Calvin, why didn't you want to be on Safety Patrol? I think you would have been a fine candidate for it."

"Oh, I just didn't want to be in the spotlight and tell others what to do. Most kids were too bossy last year, and I decided I didn't want to be like that."

Mrs. Walton said, "Well, you could just be yourself and still do a great job."

I said, "Sorry, Safety Patrol is not for me," and I walked away. In my head I just knew it was really because I didn't want to be judged or teased by anyone. Especially by any of the unkind kids. Some of them were impulsive, unpredictable and downright mean. I just wanted to steer clear of as many problems as I could.

After recess, Mrs. Walton announced the students selected for the Safety Patrol. The selected students had a variety of personalities. A few smart kids (Ashley Anderson, Tia Rainey, and Roosevelt Carter), a few quiet kids (Daryl Winthrop, and Brandon Jones), and a few kids who played around a lot (Daniel Garcia, Sammy Smith and Ava Johansson). I'm guessing there weren't many applicants or Mrs. Walton thought Safety Patrol would be good for some of these students' self-esteem. That's probably why she wanted me to be on it.

At the end of the day, there was a school wide assembly to introduce the new Safety Patrol. Each student on the Patrol had their name called and they walked up on stage to receive their sash and badge. The teachers took turns talking about the school rules and the expectations of the Safety Patrol. They also emphasized what each student could do to help out in school and how they could go to a Safety Patrol member if they ever needed help. Mrs. Walton's speech was very motivational and, secretly, I wished I was now on that stage wearing the sash and badge.

I decided at this moment that it was me who was holding me back from being courageous. I'm going to have to step things up.

3 Jealousy

The next morning, as the students walked through the halls to go to their classrooms, the Safety Patrol members were stationed at their posts. At the very front of school, I walked by Ashley and she gave me a smug look as if to say, "I'm better than you." I kept walking. Next, I came upon Tia who was tying a first grader's shoe. The other little kids around her were mesmerized by her helpfulness and bright yellow sash with the shiny silver badge. One kid was even touching it. I could tell the kids looked up to Tia as she was a kind person. Deep down I felt jealous.

As I began to walk down the third, fourth, and fifth grade hallway, I saw Daryl Winthrop helping a third grader pick up her books. I heard him say, "Be careful when you turn the corners because you don't know when someone is coming the other way. Everyone is supposed to stay to the right side of the hallway, but that doesn't always happen."

The girl said, "Thank you," and was on her way. In my head I couldn't believe Daryl was actually doing a nice job. Again, I felt a bit jealous that I wasn't on the Safety Patrol.

I walked down the hall closer to my class and saw Daniel Garcia on one knee. Behind him was Vinnie Wood yelling, "You're not going to tell me what to do!" I then saw Brandon Jones run into Mr. Sampson's fourth grade classroom. Mr. Sampson came out into the hallway and saw what was happening. As Daniel got up, he started to charge like a bull toward Vinney. Mr. Sampson stepped right in his path and Daniel crashed into his leg and then fell to the floor again. I then heard Vinney say, "I don't know how you were picked for Safety Patrol." I guess this was Vinney's way of showing jealousy. While, at the same time, this was the kind of problem that I thought I would have if I were a Safety Patrol member.

I think that many of the regular students were a little jealous of the Safety Patrol but were afraid to admit it. However, avoiding problems was the goal of many of our students on a daily basis. There was a lot of unspoken pressure while walking through the halls, eating lunch, playing on recess or walking home from school. At any given moment, anyone could have a bully or teasing target on their back. Avoiding problems was something that was never discussed, but it was a big part of school. We also figured out that jealousy was a strong emotion. We didn't talk about it in class so, like many other emotions, we would have to navigate it on our own.

If you were a fly on the wall at Wash El (that's what some people called Washington Elementary for short) you'd see some questionable choices kids made on a daily basis. We all tried to find our social order within our classrooms and grade levels. It was a never-ending battle of, "Who could outdo who?" There were the smart kids who were selfish and downright mean to anyone who challenged them through correction or by scoring higher on a test. There were quiet kids who just tried to blend in and stay away from problems. There were a few "button pushers" who tried to control others by getting them to react to an unkind word or action. There were the "bully stoppers" who were the more courageous kids, who would occasionally step in if they heard a bully causing problems. If you weren't a bully then you wanted a bully stopper to be on your side. The bullies were the kids trying to prove their self-worth by putting others down in order to make themselves feel good. A social status list was never talked about, but it must have been in some students' heads. Several times a day someone was trying to seek attention in the wrong way by showing off, teasing, or being mean. The students who tried to climb the imaginary list were successful in their own minds, while their actions were viewed as unsuccessful in other students' minds.

Lenny Dale was a short blonde-haired boy who was from the Southern Pines neighborhood but recently moved to the Vineyard Apartments. I didn't think much of it but kind of wondered why he moved. He was now happy and bragging that he lived closer to school than anyone and could be home watching TV before the rest of us crossed Bishop Boulevard. Most of the kids ignored his happiness and bragging. Harold Hutchens, who could easily turn mean whenever he wanted, saw Lenny's happiness as a chance to up his social status by bringing Lenny down.

We were walking to art class in a near perfect single file line. Mrs. Walton demanded her lines be exceptional as we were the school leaders now and other classes looked up to us. I heard Harold, who was a few students behind me in line, mumble to Lenny, "Even though you live closer to school now, you're no better than the rest of us." I don't think Lenny did or said anything, but I was in front of both of them and I wouldn't dare look back in fear of breaking Mrs. Walton's proud line formation. Then I heard it. The sound of "crunch" followed by another "crunch." It was a double flat tire sound that we all knew too well. In my mind I thought right away it must have been Harold stepping on the backs of Lenny's heels. I then heard the words, "Ah, man," coming from Lenny, followed by Mrs. Walton's very loud command "Halt!" The line stopped in unison on a dime. Almost everyone looked back over their shoulder to see Lenny on the floor trying to pull up the heels of both sneakers with little success. These were serious flat tires. He needed to untie them to put them back on. I caught a glimpse of Harold who was standing behind Lenny looking up at the third-grade artwork on the wall. I wondered in my head, *was Harold interested in art or was he guilty of this no-good act upon Lenny?* This was a 'no brainer.' He was definitely guilty of administering the double flat tire.

Eddie Monroe was behind Harold with a smile on his face. Mrs. Walton went back to Eddie and pulled his elbow and dragged him up to the front of the line. We all waited in stillness and silence.

I could hear Mrs. Walton's powerful whisper, "I know you know, so tell me, what happened back there."

Without hesitation Eddie said, "Harold gave Lenny double flat tires." Mrs. Walton went back to Harold and looked at him.

Harold spoke first. "It was an accident. I didn't mean to step on his heels."

Mrs. Walton said, "Well, then what should you be doing now?"

"I guess say I'm sorry?" Harold questioned.

"Not to me," Mrs. Walton said.

Harold looked at Lenny, who was still struggling on the floor, and said, "I'm sorry your shoes fell off." At that very moment, Mrs. Walton grabbed Harold's left ear and walked him up to the front of the line. Silence continued. We then began walking the rest of the way to art class.

As we went into the art room, Harold said the word, "snitch" to Eddie. It was followed by a threatening, "You're next."

I could see the uncomfortable look on Eddie's face. He didn't look too good. I do think this was the first time a lot of us heard the word "snitch." The word must have just been invented. We certainly knew what it meant now.

Harold then said, "You cost me my recess, Eddie." Eddie was now the victim and all he did was answer the teacher's question. I'm so glad I wasn't in line behind Harold. Then I thought to myself, *how does telling the truth turn into snitching, followed by looking over one's shoulder and knowing you are the next victim?*

My mind raced further as I wondered, *Would I have stepped in to help protect Eddie if he was a good kid? Harold was about a foot shorter than me so I wasn't scared of him. His unpredictable and crazy behavior might have been a challenge. It's a good thing Eddie is not a very kind kid because I'm not sure I'm ready to get into other people's troubles. Maybe this is another sign that I'm still not cut out for being courageous.*

Whatever the case may be, I do know that, "snitching" was not a learning objective in school, but it looks as though any kid should learn and understand it. Thanks for the lesson, Eddie.

5 Unshowy

There were two things that didn't sit well with me: bullying and being wrong in front of a large group. The feeling I got from either was uncomfortable. I didn't mind when bullies bullied each other, but I did mind when they bothered innocent students. I'm confident I will stand up to a bully soon, I think.

Although I felt like I was cautiously developing more courage, I still would not raise my hand to answer a question in front of a large group.

Mrs. Walton knew my issue. When she asked the class a question, hands would immediately go up all around. She would look at me almost every time to see if I would raise my hand. I never did. She called me up to her desk one time to speak about why I wouldn't answer her questions. I told her the truth, that I didn't want to be wrong in front of the others.

Mrs. Walton said, "But I know you know the answers." Mrs. Walton told me she wanted to talk about this with my mom.

I said, "That's fine, I think she knows how I am." As I walked away, my mind raced with things I should have said. *I know I wasn't the only one who didn't raise their hand in class. Others were like me. Most of the non-hand raisers just wanted to be quiet and, if at all possible, not draw attention to ourselves. In our minds, answering a question in front of our peers was not worth the chance of being wrong and getting teased.*

Upon talking with my mom, I found out that Mrs. Walton has been trying to understand me better and get more out of me. She just wanted to make me feel more comfortable in front of a large group.

I said, "I'm doing pretty well in her class. I am at the top of the class in handwriting and near the top in spelling and math."

Mom said, "I think she wants you to talk more. I told her about what you like to do and that you were a pretty good swimmer."

The next day Mrs. Walton assigned us an oral report about something we were good at doing. Something we were passionate about. I went home and asked my mom if she had anything to do with this assignment and of course she said no. The oral reports would start at the end of the week.

Myself, along with several others, struggled to come up with a topic that we felt comfortable sharing out loud. Swimming would have been my logical choice as I was one of the top kids in my age group during summer swim league. I also knew that some kids in our class didn't know how to swim. I knew I would feel awkward bragging about my swimming skill. So, I chose kickball as my topic.

On speech day, I was nervous. I did stumble on my words a few times. I had a beginning, middle and end so I felt like I followed the instructions.

Later on, that day Mrs. Walton asked, "Why didn't you choose swimming as your topic?"

I told her, "Most of the kids knew I was passionate about swimming. I didn't want to seem like I was bragging. Especially since some kids in our class have not ever had the chance to swim."

I think she understood, but there was another reason. I felt weird knowing that the 'Bloomers' pool I belonged to was in between

Wellington Heights and Southern Pines neighborhoods. Some of the kids from school who didn't belong to the Bloomers pool would come and stand outside of the barbed wire chain link fence and watch the swim meets. They saw me being a successful swimmer. I had a hard time being separated from my classmates by a barbed wire fence. I would talk through the fence with them during the meets, and they were always happy to see me. I told them to come inside and sit with me, but they never did.

After the speeches were over, you could say that there were definitely some braggers in our class. Those who were bragging were looked down upon by the student audience. You could hear some smirks during some of the reports. Without realizing it, some students may have even put the teasing or bullying target on their own backs. My kickball speech seemed to blend right in. I was unshowy and away from being the target.

Once in a while during recess, we would play on the far end of the playground near the back side of the school. We would walk up the hill through the pine tree area to get to the back field. The lowest branches of the pine trees were about eight feet from the ground so we could walk through the small pine tree forest without having to duck. You could actually see from the blacktop/kickball area through the pine trees from the back field. A recess lady would have to come up to the field with us because we were too far away from the usual playing area.

Today we had a group of eight kids who wanted to play tag, so we got permission and headed up to the field. The field was surrounded on two sides by the school, one side by woods, and one side by a street which had an old building facing the school. We thought it was some sort of hospital. Some people even said it was the original Washington Elementary School. It was a Victorian style building that looked pretty run down. Whenever we were up there, we always saw adults coming and going from the building and didn't think much of it.

As we arrived in the field, I noticed a group of three men standing outside of the building and looking over at our tag game. It was a little strange, so I kept an eye out once in a while when I wasn't being chased. I could see the men were smoking cigarettes. We could also smell the smoke from them when the wind blew our way.

Then it happened. As if it were in slow motion, I saw one of the guys flick the remains of his cigarette into the air towards our field. The orange tip was glowing and a few sparks flew outward. Then it bounced onto the dry grass at the edge of our field. At first my heart seemed to skip a beat, then I collected myself. I casually walked up to Mrs. Brown, our recess lady, and told her what I saw. The kids all gathered around, and some of them said they saw it too. Mrs. Brown told us not to look at them. I had to look. The three men were still standing there looking back at us to see what we were doing or what we were going to do.

Mrs. Brown had a plan. She told Lenny and Eileen to run together around the building toward the playground. When they turned the corner and were out of sight they should stop. The men will see you run, think you are telling on them, and they will go away.

"Now go," said Mrs. Brown. Lenny and Eileen took off like deer. My heart was pounding in my chest. Sure enough, as Lenny and Eileen turned the corner, we looked over and saw the three men walking away quickly toward the back of their building. Her plan worked! Mrs. Brown led the rest of us over to the edge of the field and stomped out the cigarette and the small grass fire that was just starting.

When we got inside, we were so excited to tell Mrs. Walton about how Mrs. Brown saved the day.

Mrs. Walton said, "We should give her an award." Then she also sent myself and Tia to tell Principal Donnelly about what happened and to have him ask Mr. Billy, our custodian, to re-check the field.

It turned out that, when Mr. Billy went out to the field, the fire had started up again. Thankfully, he reported that he was able put it out. I felt proud and courageous to be a first responder in a real emergency situation. Myself, Mrs. Brown, Eileen, Lenny, Tia, Mrs. Walton, Mr. Donnelly and Mr. Billy all worked as a team. Our field and possibly our school were saved!

7 Nosebleed

I don't know why I felt embarrassed when I got the occasional nosebleed because other people got them too. My nosebleeds were from dry air or pollen flying around during the change of seasons. Also, my nose might bleed if I blew it too hard. I could never really anticipate when a nosebleed would show up. Just in case, I started carrying a tissue in my pocket. Whenever I got a nosebleed at school, I was able to catch it early enough, go to the bathroom, and get it to stop.

Today, Mrs. Walton had beautiful flowers on her desk. They were a gift from her husband celebrating their wedding anniversary. I sat near the front so I could actually smell the flowers. They smelled pretty good. Without even thinking of what might happen, I sneezed. Luckily, I had a tissue in my back pocket so I was prepared. I quickly found out that a hard sneeze also made my nose bleed. I pinched my nose while holding the tissue right away, but some blood was already running down my hand. Because Mrs. Walton did not like interruptions, I hardly ever spoke out of turn, but this moment was an exception.

I got out of my seat, walked up to Mrs. Walton's desk and asked, "Can I go to the nurse?"

She said, "Of course, and keep your nose pinched all the way there."

As I turned to walk to the door, I heard a few people making noises.

Ashley blurted out, "Eww, that looks gross."

I tried to ignore her and the class noises, but I still felt embarrassed. I kept walking toward the classroom door.

Then I heard Vinney say, "Just tell the nurse I hit you. I was probably going to do it any way. You just beat me to it." That was his idea of humor. I just looked at him and kept walking. In my mind, it was a lame attempt to get the class to give him attention. Several kids nearby laughed at Vinnie's words and made me feel even more like a spectacle. I heard Ashley laughing too.

I was at the nurse's office for a while as it turned out to be a bad nosebleed. I missed most of my reading class. When I got back, it was time to get in line for lunch. I was toward the end of the line when Vinney walked by and said, "Are you ready for that punch in the nose now?"

Palo was behind me and said to Vinney, "Get in line." Vinney then gave Palo a mean look and held his hands out to the side. He aggressively asked, "What are you going to do about it?"

As Vinnie walked by, Palo lunged at him but didn't touch him. Vinney flinched, took a step sideways, and tripped over a chair. Then he fell on top of a desk that moved with him several feet. He slid down on one knee before he was able to stand back up again. Palo, myself, and all the kids in the area were laughing. Vinney knew he had no chance against Palo.

He just said, "Hey, what did you do that for? I was just kidding."

Mrs. Walton came to the back of the line and confronted Vinney face to face. In her unfriendliest voice she said, "You again." Vinney got in line without saying a word. He had already lost several recesses this year due to poor behavior. He knew he would lose recess again if he said anything to her.

I always felt Palo had my back, but I never knew when he would be there for me. He seemed to show up at the right times. Helping him spell words last year in fourth grade turned out to be good for me. We also played on the same basketball team, played kickball at recess and we were in the same baseball league in the summer. We had a lot in common. I was grateful for knowing Palo was on my side, and I know I will continue helping him out. I thanked him as we went out for recess. He shook his head in approval and said, "No worries, let's play some kickball." Vinney didn't say or do anything more.

8 The Target Is on Me

When I first came to school this morning, I was
feeling good. Today was our gym day. We were
also going to read to our first-grade reading
buddies this afternoon, and there was blue sky for
kickball at recess time.

As I made my way to my seat, the students
were talking out loud as usual.

Ashley, who was selfish and never very
kind, came up to me and boldly said, "Your breath
really stinks. Do you brush your teeth?"

Those words hurt, but I responded anyway,
"Yes. I brush every day."

Then she said, "Your high-top sneakers are
bobo's."

I said, "Look around, half the class has
them. You will be getting them soon."

She said, "No I will not."

Then I walked away and sat down.

From that point on, I became quiet. I didn't
want to talk and have others say what she said.
Ashley was mean, and she meant to make me feel

bad. Her words sure did change my day. However, her words were actually the spark I needed. I decided then and there that I would stand up for myself and others whenever necessary. Without getting into trouble, from now on I plan to get Ashley back whenever she tries to bully me or anyone else.

I did become self-conscious for a while until I remembered I had nose problems. My doctor had told me that my nose septum was twisted, and I was allergic to dust and pollen. I also recall him saying there was no real cure, so just keep some breath mints in your pocket.

On that same day at recess, Chucky McManus was the captain of my kickball team. I was usually pretty good at kickball and got on base most of the time. On my second kick, I flied out to Vinnie in center field and Chucky was not happy.

When I came into our bench area, he said, "You know you have duck feet."

I said, "What are you talking about?"

He said, "When you walk or run your feet turn way out like a duck. We should call you duck man."

I just scowled at him and said, "No, that's not cool," as I walked away to the back of the kicking line.

After this second bodily scarring, I thought I must have a target on my back today. I amused myself by looking over my shoulder and pulling at my shirt to see.

Now, I tried to stay quiet and keep my feet inward when I walked or ran. I didn't want to be told I had bad breath and be called a duck man again. Fortunately, nobody else picked up on my duck-like feet and the nickname never stuck. It was, however, hard not to speak and to keep my feet straight all the time.

After two painful experiences, I was just hoping to get through the rest of the day without any more teasing or name calling. Unfortunately, I guess things do happen in groups of three.

On our way to the first-grade room for reading buddies, Eddie said, "You know what Calvin, you look like a toad. We should make that your new nickname." Eddie smiled, but I didn't.

I said to him, "I don't think I need a nickname, please do not call me that." Eddie started doing it more.

I towered over little Eddie with my muscles tense. I calmly said, "I thought we were good. This is my second request. Can you please stop calling me toad?"

Eddie, with a fake grin, pretended it was funny, but I didn't. Just before school was let out while we were packing up to go home, Eddie called me toad again. This time I went over to Mrs. Walton and told her what he's been doing. I told her that I asked him to stop two times, but he wouldn't.

Mrs. Walton called him over and told him, "When someone says stop you must honor their request and stop. Calvin has asked you to stop calling him toad. What should you do now?"

Eddie said, "I will stop."

Mrs. Walton said, "Calvin, let me know if it happens again."

As we walked home, Eddie said, "You're a snitch." I smiled and nodded at him but didn't say anything. Besides the fact that I was a foot taller than him, I think my non response helped him understand it was over. He then cowardly ran ahead and walked with another group of kids.

Today was my day to feel how mean words felt. It definitely was a day that knocked me down a few spots on my imaginary social ladder. I thought maybe it was all a good lesson for me. This day had to be my turning point for showing my courage. I decided to take the high road today and put today's bullying behind me. In fact, those words were on one of Mrs. Walton's words of wisdom posters.

It read: *Stay optimistic, stay driven, and when you have a choice on which way to go, take the high road.*

As I turned the corner on my way home, I remembered what my older sister Clare used to say.

She said, "Mean kids who say mean things are helping you to develop thick skin. You just have to take it and move on. Responding to their mean words only makes things worse. "

I guessed Clare's 'move on' message was like 'take the high road' on the poster. I thought my actions and those words were somewhat similar today.

Ashley has had it out for me, and I won't forget what she said. She doesn't realize it, but I will stand up to her from now on.

Chucky just cannot stand to lose which I understand. I'm sure we will both move on. If not, I will stand up to him too.

Eddie is stuck being bullied and trying to bully others. He is often picked on and was trying to make himself feel better by bringing my emotions down. I get that too, but I'm not going to be his victim.

Today didn't feel good, and I know I won't forget it. The target was on me. I guess it was just my turn. In the end, I did feel my courage was coming.

9 The Talk

On Monday morning, we were given a form letter which explained the "Growing up" lesson that was going to be held this coming Friday. "The Talk," is what we called it and it would be a memorable time for all of us. The two fifth grade classes would be split into two groups. One would be made up of all the boys and the other group would be all of the girls. The boys would go with the PE teacher, Mr. Howard, and learn about male and female body parts while the girls would go with the school nurse to do the same. The form was to be returned only if a parent did not want their child to participate in the lesson. The signed non consent form was to be returned by Thursday of this week. If you were not going to the lecture, you had to sit in the library and read. I guessed a few kids' parents might not want their child to hear about this sensitive topic, and I also guessed that some kids wouldn't bother to take the form home.

During Friday morning's homeroom, one could sense an extra air of enthusiasm among our classmates. Before we took our seats to begin class, I could hear a few kids commenting on today's main event.

"I can't wait. This is going to be great," said Roosevelt.

Then I heard Palo say, "I'm a little nervous."

That sounded odd coming from the biggest and strongest kid in the class. Maybe he was just kidding. Some of the girls were giggling and blushing in a group, but I couldn't hear what they were saying.

I did hear Ashley say to another girl, "Did you hear? Hellen Matters is not allowed to go."

I then wondered if any boys weren't going. All day long my mind thought about what might happen this afternoon in today's growing up lesson. At recess time, I saw Christopher Sanchez standing against the school wall doing recess detention. James told me he heard that Christopher asked Ashley if she knew what planet rhymed with a male body part? She immediately told Mrs. Walton and, within seconds, Christopher was assigned recess detention. I laughed out loud when James told me. I knew what he said to her was wrong, but I was laughing because of how foolish Christopher had been. I have to admit that it was also funny he asked Ashley that question.

After recess, all of our boys lined up with Ms. Joseph's fifth grade boys in the hallway. Our girls all went into Ms. Joseph's class and sat down to wait for the school Nurse. Mrs. Walton walked all of the boys to the gym. I hoped she wouldn't be staying with us during the lecture because that would be embarrassing.

Mr. Howard had the chairs spread out about five feet apart within each row. Clearly, he didn't want us talking to our neighbors during the lesson.

He said, "You all need to be quiet, raise your hand to speak, and do not draw attention to yourself by fooling around or laughing. If you do break any of these rules, you will have to sit in the hallway and not learn what fifth graders are supposed to know. If you are disruptive by laughing, it just means that you are not mature enough for this lesson. You will have to catch up on what you miss in sixth grade."

The first picture that he put on the overhead projector had a drawing of a naked male. I could see most of the boys were holding back laughter. Mr. Howard wrinkled his forehead and scowled at us. The next picture he put up had labels that gave the proper name for all of the male body parts. Mr. Howard read them out loud. Some boys snickered again. Mr. Howard scowled again. Mrs. Walton was sitting in the front next to the screen. She started scowling back at all of the boys who were making noise. The pictures were embarrassing, but somehow, I held my laughter inside. The final male picture had an older male with more body hair.

Mr. Howard said, "This guy represents how your body will be changing in the next few years." The final male picture reminded us to shower or bathe regularly and use deodorant every day.

Next up, Mr. Howard put a drawing of a naked girl on the overhead projector. Much louder snickering noises came out of some of the kids. I could also see some boys bending forward in their seats while laughing and holding their stomachs. Brandon Jones was one of those boys. He just could not stop laughing, so Mrs. Walton grabbed his elbow and walked him out to the hallway where he sat for the rest of the lesson. As she returned, everyone was silent again. The next image had the same naked girl with her body parts labeled. Mr. Howard read all the body parts out loud. He also said we would be learning about the reproductive system in sixth grade. Today was an introduction to the proper terminology for the male and female body parts.

We were then asked if we had any questions. Vinney blurted out, "How do you make a baby?" Many of the boys laughed out loud at that question.

Mr. Howard said, "That's what the reproductive system is all about. You can find out next year in sixth grade health class or, if you really want to know, ask your parents when you get home. Our curriculum for fifth grade is an introduction to body parts and hygiene. Remember all of you should be showering or bathing regularly, wearing clean clothes and putting on deodorant every day."

As we walked out, Mr. Howard handed each of us a small deodorant stick.

He said, "Take this home and start using it." He also said, "You should not talk about our lesson on your way home, as younger kids are immature and not ready to learn what fifth graders know."

Vinney called out, "Except for Brandon! He is an immature fifth grader sitting in the hallway who missed out."

Mr. Howard didn't have an answer, and we all took turns receiving our new deodorant stick. I asked, "Can I have one for Brandon?" Mr. Howard gave me a second one as we walked toward the door.

Upon entering the hallway, Vinney was in front of me and started laughing and pointing at Brandon, "Ha, ha, ha, you were not mature enough for the lesson. You missed it."

My heart raced as I spoke up and said, "Leave him alone."

Vinney, turned back, looked up (I was now five inches taller than him) and asked, "What are you going to do about it?"

As he had his head turned upwards toward me waiting for an answer, he walked backward into Palo who was stopped in front of him. He bounced back as though he had walked into a wall. He fell back into me and bounced back into Palo. It was as if we were playing ping pong with him.

Palo shoved him and asked, "What's your problem Vinney?"

Vinney, who was outsized and outwitted, said, "Oh, no problem, I'm good."

Palo said, "Oh no you're not. You stink. You should put that deodorant on now."

Some kids nearby in the line chuckled.

I then circled around to the back of the line and gave Brandon his deodorant.

Brandon said, "Thanks Calvin. I appreciate you standing up to Vinney. I know I shouldn't have gotten kicked out, but I just couldn't stop laughing."

I said, "I know how it is. I laugh uncontrollably once in a while too."

When we got back to class, the girls and boys wanted to know what happened in each other's lecture. It was dismissal time, so not too many details were shared. I did hear that Eileen Dottson started to get sick and had to leave the girls' lesson. My newly acquired knowledge of human body parts did make me feel a little more grown up. Speaking up to Vinnie also helped my courage grow. I felt like the boys in my class were now looking at me in a more positive way, and I liked it.

The school let out and we all walked toward Bishop Boulevard and waited to cross. It seemed to me that my fellow fifth graders were not fooling around as usual. Maybe they also had the same grown up feeling I had from the lesson. As I walked, I also felt about two inches taller and stronger for standing up to Vinney. He walked nearby but didn't say a word to me. The walk home was problem free.

10 Balderdash!

As my good friend James and I walked into the school building today, nothing seemed out of the ordinary. We could hear and see the usual sounds of students buzzing around and getting ready for the day. Our classrooms were at the far end of the hall which seemed like a football field's length away. The exterior door at the end of the hallway looked about the size of a quarter. We could see the sunlight beams shining in.

The usual sounds of kids talking, lockers shutting and feet shuffling were all of a sudden drowned out by someone yelling the word, "Balderdash!"

This word was so loud and powerful that it seemed to shake the hallway. I really didn't know what it meant, but I could tell it didn't sound like a word of approval. That unmistakable voice was coming from my teacher, Mrs. Walton.

Every day we had a morning routine of handing in our homework to Mrs. Walton. She would check it quickly and put it into a pile. Later on in the day she would put a note on them and place them back into our mailboxes. I found out when I got to class that Eddie didn't have his homework. He said his dog ate it. That's when Mrs. Walton yelled that unforgettable, forceful, hallway shaking word. Even though we didn't exactly know what the word meant, we quickly figured out that this word was the one word you did not want her to say to you. Later during recess, I saw Eddie sitting against the school doing his homework.

That afternoon, during our social studies class with Ms. Joseph (her students were with Mrs. Walton for Science), Harold Hutchens was throwing sunflower seeds at Ava Johansson who was minding her own business. Most of the class could see it happening, but Ms. Joseph could not catch him as he only did it when she was not looking. It looked like he had a pocket full of the seeds.

After about four throws and one seed stuck in her hair, Ava turned around and said, "Please stop!" Ms. Joseph heard this and asked Ava what she was trying to stop.

Ava said, "Someone is throwing sunflower seeds at me." It seemed like everyone in the room looked at Harold who was now staring out of the window.

Ava then said, "I think it's Harold." Ms. Joseph asked for a show of hands to see if anyone saw Harold throw seeds at Ava. Four girls who were sitting near Harold raised their hands. Ms. Joseph sent a disgruntled Harold out to sit in the hallway.

When the lessons ended, we lined up ready to cross the hall and go back to our own classrooms. As we passed the other class, some kids gave high fives while others avoided each other. Harold was sitting against a locker as if to be waiting for the judge for his trial. We actually had been learning about the legal system in social studies class. He must have known what was coming.

Our class sat down quickly and quietly because we wanted to hear Mrs. Walton's interrogation. You could hear a pin drop as everyone leaned an ear toward the open classroom door. We could hear Ms. Joseph explain what happened. Then it was Harold's turn.

He said, "I didn't throw nothing at anyone."

Mrs. Walton corrected Harold. "That's anything."

She then said, "Now please stand up. What did they say you were throwing?"

Harold said, "Sunflower seeds."

Mrs. Walton said, "Like those on the floor where you were just sitting?"

Harold said, "Those aren't mine."

It seemed like time stood still for the next second as we anticipated the word that was coming next.

"Balderdash!" yelled Mrs. Walton.

Then, with a voice so calm you could soothe a baby with, Mrs. Walton said, "You and I will be spending some quality time together at recess."

11 Bathroom in the Classroom

Each day before we went into the classroom, we dropped off our books, lunch box (if you packed) and jacket in our hallway locker. You only walked into the classroom with your homework and reading book. You were also expected to walk straight to your desk after turning in your homework. Mrs. Walton was no nonsense and very punctual about starting class on time. If you needed to use the bathroom, it was located to the right of the doorway when you entered the classroom.

I was embarrassed to use the bathroom. I think I just didn't want to use it because I felt weird that my peers would be so close by. Other kids had no problem using it. Just out of curiosity, I kept a list of who used the bathroom. There were only eight kids in our class who actually used the bathroom in the classroom. My chosen places to relieve myself were at home, in the hallway bathroom during special class, or the cafeteria bathroom. The other kids who wouldn't use the in-class bathroom also had the same plan.

One boy in particular had no problem going to the bathroom in the classroom. His name was Franny Lutz. Today, I noticed he went in there before Mrs. Walton started class. The rule was that you could go in at any time as long as nobody else was using it.

Mrs. Walton had started our morning routine so I kind of forgot Franny was even in there. Finally, he came out and walked to his seat. I checked the clock and calculated that he was in there for about ten minutes. Nobody said anything, but you could see kids who were seated in the back near the bathroom smiling or grimacing. Some were also waving their hands in front of their noses as if to clear the air they were breathing. Anyone could see by their actions that the odor smelled bad.

Franny had left the door open after he came out. This was an expected practice so others knew the bathroom was available to use. The kids who sat near the bathroom did indeed smell something awful and Daryl Winthrop called out, "Good God that really stinks." I don't think Mrs. Walton heard him or she just ignored him because she knew what was happening. There was a thick cloud of number two foul smell in the air.

Vinnie raised his hand and Mrs. Walton called on him. "Yes, Vinnie."

"Mrs. Walton, can I open up the windows? It stinks back here."

I don't know how she kept a straight face as kids held back pure laughter with slight giggling sounds. Some students put their heads down, so Mrs. Walton wouldn't see them laughing. I was holding a straight face for as long as I could, but I had to put my head down and let it out. At that point I couldn't stop laughing. I wasn't laughing too loud, but my stomach was in convulsions and tears were coming from my eyes. Finally, Mrs. Walton said, "Calvin, go to the hallway, settle yourself, and come back when you are ready."

I laughed all the way to the door while the kids watched me. I could hardly get a breath in because I was laughing so hard. I don't know how kids were just smiling. I was holding my sides and bent over laughing as I walked toward the door. I seemed to be the only one who couldn't stop laughing. When I was getting ready to exit the room, I stopped, took a whiff and swung my hand in front of my face that was wet from my tears of laughter. While Daryl pinched his nose shut, he whispered to me in a duck sounding voice, "You're lucky you get to leave."

As soon as I got into the hallway, I dove down on the ground laughing and crying at the same time. My eyes were closed and my stomach was convulsing with a crazy roller coaster feeling. As I lay on my back, I opened my eyes and a third-grade class was standing on the other side of the hallway waiting to go outside. They all starred at me like I had something wrong. They were right. I did manage to sit up against the lockers, take a deep breath, wipe the tears off my cheeks and stop laughing. Now my face was flushed, and I was just smiling. They all continued to look at me as they walked by to go outside.

I finally got myself together and went back into the classroom. As I walked to my seat, I knew not to look at Franny. That might trigger another laughing fit. I sat down and got to work on a reading worksheet.

I noticed later at lunch and recess that kids were going up to Franny and talking to him. He just had a grin from ear to ear and held his stomach as if to be proud of himself. I stayed away. I wasn't great friends with Franny, so I certainly didn't need to strike up a conversation about what happened.

I made it through the rest of the day without any more bouts of laughter. When I met up with James on the walk home, he brought up the incident.

I said, "Come on James, please don't get me started."

James said, "Dude, I could smell it from our room across the hallway. What was he eating?"

I busted out laughing again and managed to ask, "James, can we please talk about something else?"

James said, "Well, I'd like to be a fly on the wall during your morning meeting tomorrow. I imagine that will be interesting."

The next day, all the kids went through their usual routine prior to the morning meeting. I stopped at my locker, put my lunch away and entered the class. The door to the bathroom was wide open and there was no smell. I sat down next to Ava, who was also a big laugher, and asked her how she was doing.

In her Swedish accent she said, "Fine thanks. I see you survived yesterday."

I said, "Yeah, I'm good."

Mrs. Walton was about to start class.

She said, "For our class meeting today we are having a discussion about bathroom etiquette. It was so hard for me to keep a straight face. Ashley had her hand up already.

Mrs. Walton reluctantly asked, "What is it, Ashley?"

Ashley said, "I think we should make a rule that the boys must pick the seat up before they go to the bathroom. Most of the time, when they leave it down, they urinate on it. Also, after they pick the seat up to urinate, they should put it back down before they leave. That would be bathroom etiquette."

I don't know what came over me, but it was probably Ashley's smug tone of voice. I blurted out,

"Hold on, that would mean the boys would have to move the seat two times to the girl's zero times. That is definitely not fair. Plus, most every girl and boy probably wipe the seat before they sit down anyway."

Mrs. Walton would usually stop the students who called out, but she seemed shocked from what Ashley requested and let my equally surprising reply go.

Ashley continued, "We have etiquette at my house and the boys raise and lower the seat when they urinate. That's how it should be done here."

I said, "No, the boys can pick the seat up, but the girls should at least put it down. That is a good compromise."

Mrs. Walton heard enough and yelled out, "Halt, that's it!" You could hear a pin drop.

She said, "Well class, we are going to end this right now. Sorry Ashley, but Calvin is right. His plan makes it fair for everyone. The boys will pull the seat up and the girls will put the seat down. We will try it out for a while. If it does not work, everyone will have to sit down all the time and nobody will move the seat. Case dismissed." She then banged a wooden mallet onto her wooden desk for added emphasis. Girls were shaking their heads in disbelief, but Mrs. Walton was the judge and she made the ruling.

Ashley raised her hand again. Mrs. Walton did not look happy.

She said, ``What is it now, Ashley?"

Ashley said, "We still need to discuss the terrible smell the bathroom sends out when someone goes number two and leaves the door open." The room was silent. Some kids looked at Mrs. Walton, some looked at Franny who was smiling again, and some stared with surprised looks at Ashley.

Mrs. Walton said, "To avoid a lengthy discussion from now on, if you go number two, you shut the door when you come out."

I was still feeling bold, and without hesitation I said, "...and then we can put a sign up that says, Enter at your own risk." Some kids had their mouths wide open and sat in shock while others laughed out loud.

Mrs. Walton said, "Well Calvin, you certainly have developed some courage, but this time it will cost you. For calling out during the morning meeting, you will be giving up your recess. Morning meeting adjourned." Ashley smiled at me as if she got me. I moved my hand to grab an imaginary toilet seat, and then put it down. Then with a fake smile, I gave her a thumbs down sign.

At the end of the day, Mrs. Walton announced, "Boys and girls, we will have a new student named Mary Heelman joining our class tomorrow. You should all know that she is legally blind."

The class started mumbling toward one another and hands immediately went up.

Andrew couldn't wait and called out, "How much can she see? Does she have a guide cane?"

Mrs. Walton said, "Ok everyone hands down. Let me give you more information. She does have a guide cane, but she will need some additional help. Try to help her only when she needs it. Mary can see a little out of one eye and can do some things on her own. We should allow her to be independent whenever possible."

Lenny spoke up and said, "What does legally blind mean?"

Mrs. Walton actually responded to his calling out.

"Good question. It means that she cannot read the largest letter on an eye chart like we can." She went on to say, "Everyone close your eyes and open one just a little bit. This is about what Mary can see. She will need help walking from place to place. I spoke with Tia about this already, and she will be Mary's guide."

Tia was one of the most responsible kids in the class, but many kids didn't like how perfect she was at everything. Nobody argued Mrs. Walton's choice, but one might think Tia was chosen because of being a favorite. She was definitely smart, responsible, a tattletale, and somewhat of a teacher's pet. Some days she seemed like she wanted to be the teacher and tried to tell us what to do. Usually, she was right.

The next day, just after our morning meeting, Principal Donnelly walked Mary Heelman into our classroom. Mr. Donnelly said, "Say hello to Mary everyone." In unison we all said, "Hi Mary." I thought that was slightly weird, and it looked like Mary was a little embarrassed. As we all stared at Mary, Tia guided her to a seat near the teacher's desk.

I could see Mary holding her book about two inches from one of her eyes. I thought that was a difficult way to live. I felt sorry for her. When it was time to go to special class, Tia would stand next to Mary's desk. Mary would stand up and place her hand on Tia's shoulder. Then they would walk to the line. On gym day, Tia would take Mary to the library.

During recess, Tia walked Mary around for a while and described what was going on. Then I saw a group of girls huddled around Mary and Tia. They were too far away for me to hear what they were saying, but they were certainly not giving Mary her space like Mrs. Walton suggested.

Shortly after the girl gathering, I noticed Eddie and Sammy running from behind Mary, stopping, and swinging their hands in front of her face before running away. I was trying to focus on our kickball game, but I couldn't help notice that they did this several times.

The second or third time I heard Tia yell, "Leave us alone!" They seemed to stop, but less than a minute went by, and I saw them do it again. Tia was clearly unhappy. I could also see Mary move her head away as she probably could see their hands shaking in front of her face. I ran over and told the recess lady what the boys were doing.

She went over to the boys, scolded them, and they stopped. Soon after that, the recess whistle blew and we all got in our class line to go inside.

While we were standing in line, Tia walked down the line leaving Mary in the front. She stopped next to Eddie and Sammy, pointed at them and announced, "I'm going to tell Mrs. Walton what you were doing to Mary."

Eddie blurted out, "You better not."

I then stood out of the line and courage took over. I said, "You were wrong to be mean and should get told on. I'm telling too."

Before Eddie could say anything, Andrew who was standing behind Eddie in line said, "I saw what you were doing, and I'm also telling on both of you." You could see the boys cower after Andrew let them know of his intentions. Eddie and Sammy were silent, and Tia went back in front of the line with Mary.

For as much as the class didn't always like Tia, we were on her side for this issue. Speaking up was the right thing to do. What Eddie and Sammy did was wrong. When Mrs. Walton asked the class if they saw anyone bothering anyone during recess at least eight kids raised their hands. She then had those students write down what they saw.

Ordinarily, Andrew would not tell on someone, so for him to speak up was something new. It made sense though, as Andrew understood Mary's disability. His vision was not very good. He squinted every time that he had to concentrate because he rarely wore his thick glasses. He would often forget them at home or leave them in his locker. I know he felt sorry for Mary.

Mrs. Walton never talked about empathy, courage, or the consequences that came after her investigation, but we did see Eddie and Sammy on the wall at recess for the next two days. I felt good about telling Mrs. Walton what Eddie and Sammy did, and I was not a bit worried about them trying to get me back. I'm pretty sure Andrew felt the same way. It was also good to see the other kids raise their hands and stick up for Mary. We were all learning empathy and showing courage at the same time because we knew helping her was the right thing to do. Hopefully, Eddie and Sammy learned the same lesson, just in a different way.

They clearly needed to learn empathy more than the rest of us. At least they didn't bother Mary or Tia again.

13 Willy Robot

During science class, Mrs. Walton told us she would partner everyone up, so that we could create a unique project on a tri-fold board that would make a difference in our world. She said, "This is your chance to think outside of the box, have fun, and create something special."

She gave us the specific instructions which included a thorough description of the invention, a picture of the invention in use, and a picture that shows how it works. I was paired up with Ava who was a good artist and had some interesting ideas.

Our first task was to begin writing down notes on what we were thinking we would do. Ava and I thought of a few things: a remote-controlled robot that could drive a car, a robot that cut the grass, a robot who stopped bullies, and a robot who did the laundry. Eventually we settled on a robot who stopped bullies. We decided its name would be Willy.

At first, we couldn't figure out what the robot should look like, or how it actually stopped bullies.

Ava was really into drawing, and she just kept drawing different robots. I was busy writing down ideas for the robot instructions. We did everything on paper in a rough draft before we started our finished product on the tri-fold board.

Our plan ended up being a human size robot with antennas for ears. It traveled on wheels, moved in all directions, and responded to commands given from a remote-control device. It looked similar to one we saw cleaning a house on a cartoon television show. When a bully began bullying someone, the owner, or controller of the robot, would use the remote to roll up Willy to confront the bully. Then it would say, "Stop!" plus hold up a little stop sign. If the verbal and stop sign messages did not work, the bully would then get sprayed by bug spray which would make them run away.

On the first part of the tri-fold, we had a picture of Willy and a paragraph describing how it could move, what it could say, and what it was used for. We also added that every school should have one or two of these bully stopping robots. On the second part of the tri-fold, we had Willy traveling next to an owner with a remote control. Willy's parts were also labeled on this section of the tri-fold. On the third section, we had Willy confronting a bully, holding up a stop sign, and saying, "Stop!" The student's face had a grimacing disapproval look drawn on him. Below that, we had a picture of Willy spraying the bully with the bug spray as the bully started to run away.

On the day of the reports, we stood up in front of the class and explained our invention. I wasn't nervous at all because I felt confident about our efforts. Ava and I also believed our robot could change the world. Some of the class seemed to like it, while others thought it was funny and not at all realistic. We did get a small applause when we finished.

As we started walking back to our seats, Vinney yelled out, "That robot wouldn't stop me." Some of the class laughed. We smiled too but for a different reason. Vinney wasn't close enough to notice that the robot was already stopping him. Ava had drawn a really good picture that looked just like Vinney running from the robot's spray. The bully had blue jeans, a green t-shirt, white sneakers (these colors were the opposite of what Vinnie usually wears), and black hair, just like Vinney. He didn't notice that the bully in the picture was him. Prior to our presentation, Ava and I swore never to tell anyone who the bully was on the project. As I sat down, Tia whispered to me, "That bully sure looks like Vinney running away from the robot." I just smiled, and she smiled back.

The invention displays all stood around the room for two full weeks. Besides our class looking at them, parents got to see them at parent teacher conference night. During the two weeks, a few other students told us that the bully reminded them of Vinney. We never let our secret out. Luckily, Vinney never questioned who the boy was in our drawing. When it was time to take the tri-folds down, I was relieved because I was thinking Vinney would eventually catch on. If he did figure out who the bully was, we might have wished our Willy robot was real.

Writer's workshop was another one of Mrs. Walton's passions. She would spend time instructing us on various English language writing rules and a variety of writing styles. We wrote poetry, short stories, cartoons, advertisements, autobiographies, and short fiction novels. Today she reviewed past instructions and gave additional tips on how to write a good persuasive letter.

Our challenge was to write to a twelfth grader at a nearby high school and convince them not to drink and drive during their prom night. This was the first time I ever heard of a prom. Unfortunately, it was clear that many twelfth graders made poor choices on this night. Mrs. Walton said our letters would send a powerful message to these older students.

Before we began to write, Mrs. Walton passed out the name of the person who we would be writing to. She said, our envelope contained the name of a student who lived nearest to us, and that we might even know each other. I was curious to see who I got, so I tore the envelope open right away.

At first, I did not recognize the name, Steven Shoemaker. Then his devilish smile appeared inside of my brain. I knew exactly who he was. I also knew that I didn't want to write to him. I went straight up to Mrs. Walton and asked, "Can I switch names with someone?"

Mrs. Walton asked back, "Why would you want to switch names? Explain to me what's wrong with Steven?"

I had to tell her the whole story now. I said, "Well, it happened a few weeks ago when James and I were having a catch with a baseball in my backyard. Somehow, I totally missed one of James' throws which bounced off a tree trunk and rolled toward Steven's open back door. I went over to get the ball as loud rock music blared into my ears. I scooped it up and took a quick look inside. The room had colorful flowers painted on the wall and the smell of incense burning. I also noticed a dark figure laying on the couch. I then ran back to James and told him what I saw. As we continued having our catch, two teenagers came out of nowhere and tackled us to the ground. Then as we struggled to get free, they stuffed dirty sweat socks in our mouths. When they ran away, I looked up and saw Steven and his hippie brother laughing back at us."

"Oh my!" Mrs. Walton said. "That is quite a story."

I continued, "There is more. James and I marched right to their front door and told their dad, but he didn't seem to care. He said he would talk to them, but that didn't make us feel any better. To avoid any further issues, we decided not to play in my backyard anymore. They were bigger, stronger and crazier than we were, so we thought it was best to stay away from them. I really don't want to see him again. Now, can I change names?"

Mrs. Walton said, "On the contrary, this is when you should want to speak with him. He will respect you more if you confront him with confidence versus avoiding him. You will not only write to Steven, you will get him to apologize, and best of all make him promise not to drink and drive on his prom night. Your letter will be very meaningful indeed."

Begrudgingly, I said, "Yes, Mrs. Walton, you are correct. I will keep him."

On the way home from school, I asked James if he felt this was some sort of karma getting me back for one of my wrongdoings?

James asked, "What have you done wrong lately?"

I said, "Well, I had been feeling bad for the last few weeks for the Willy Robot invention that had a picture of Vinnie getting sprayed. I've also been in constant battles with Ashley Anderson."

James said, "Well then, there you go. The sock in the mouth must have been payback for your science project and the Ashley battles. You have no worries. Your bad karma is all gone. If anything, it's Steven that has the bad vibe now."

The next day I continued writing my letter to Steven. I wrote as if I was sending a message from a spiritual leader from above. I thought his hippie attitude might be able to relate to my words. I wrote:

Dear Steven,

Even though you have already made some bad choices in life, drinking and driving could end up being your last choice. I urge you to consider what might happen if you became drunk and got behind the wheel of a car. Innocent people might get hurt if you make the wrong choice. Alcohol is not a good match for the teenage brain, and certainly not good when the teenager is behind the wheel of a car. The act of not drinking will give you positive karma. Please don't drink alcohol and drive during your prom night. From, a concerned fifth grader, CA.

A few days after we sent the letters, we got a huge surprise. The seniors who received our letters were coming to visit us in our classroom! I was a little nervous to be face to face with Steven again. When the seniors arrived, I didn't see the long-haired freaky looking dude. I thought he was probably absent. I pictured him at home laying on his couch. Then, to my surprise, a familiar face approached me.

He said, "Hello Calvin."

My heart stopped for a second. It was my neighbor, Steven, with his hair cut short enough to be in the Army.

He said, "I just want to thank you for your letter. I appreciate your advice, and I promise you I won't drink and drive."

We chatted a little more. Steven told me he was getting ready to go into the Army. I then told him about my uncle who spent time in the Vietnam War.

Feeling more confident, I had to ask, "Do you know how to do your own laundry?"

Steven said, "That's an odd question. Why would you ask that?"

I said, "The sweat sock. You remember the one you shoved in my mouth. It was pretty dirty."

He said, "Oh, yeah, I'm sorry about that. My brother and I were not thinking right that day. We promise not to do that again."

Then I asked, "Is there any chance you can turn your loud music down too?"

Steven said, "Ok, but, just so you know, my brother and I will be shipping out to boot camp right after graduation. You won't see or hear from us for a while."

I felt like Steven and I actually bonded a little and that he would take my prom advice. Mrs.

Walton was right. I believe Steven respected me more now for confronting him. I was glad I had the courage to bring up the sock incident. Although there was no consequence for his actions, Steven did seem to show a little guilt. I couldn't wait to tell James he apologized. That was better than nothing. Unfortunately, I will never forget that dirty, stinking, sweat sock taste.

15 Science Olympics

Science class was always interesting to me. I guess a few kids didn't like it as much as social studies, but I liked them both. Today, Mrs. Walton told us about a teacher in Dover, Delaware who was holding a science competition. It was called the Science Olympics. His idea came about because he thought a competition would get more students interested in science. Although his competition was only for High School students across the State, Mrs. Walton decided it would be fun to do some competitive science events within our own class.

Mrs. Walton had three events planned. They were designing and flying a model airplane for distance, building a bridge out of newspaper to hold weight, and dropping an egg from the roof of the school without it breaking. Each of us would be put on a team made up of three students. The group would work together to plan and build their projects. Then a competition would determine the class winner. The team with the highest point total for all three events would be declared the Science Olympic Champion.

Overall, the class seemed pretty psyched about it because most of the students in our class loved competitions. I was certainly all in. Mrs. Walton gave us the rules for each event. She then told us who was on our team. My teammates were Roosevelt and Eileen. I wasn't too sure how creative these two were, but I at least knew Eileen liked science and Roosevelt was competitive.

Our first day's task was to draw up plans for each activity. These plans were then to be handed in each day, so teams wouldn't take other's ideas. Our team's drawings were minimal so we decided to go home and test out a few things on our own. We would come back the next day and try them out during science class. It just so happened that each of us naturally gravitated toward one of the events. Eileen was pretty focused on the bridge building. Roosevelt was interested in making and flying the airplane, and I would focus on a plan for a safe egg drop.

The next morning, we spoke to one another about our ideas. Roosevelt said, "The airplane is ready for a test flight today."

Eileen said, "That's great! I have an idea for the bridge, but I am not too sure how strong it will be."

I replied, "We have a full week to try a few ideas. If your plan doesn't work, we can rebuild another one. As for the egg drop, we can use any container that is smaller than twelve inches long, twelve inches high and twelve inches wide. I'm thinking we pack a metal lunch box with foam around the egg for protection. That might keep the egg from breaking. The problem is that the eggs will be dropped from the top of the school to the ground, and we won't be able to test it beforehand from that height."

Eileen said, "Ok, let's talk more during recess and science. I think there are too many ears around here this morning."

Ashley was nearby, and I'm guessing she heard most of what we were talking about. I also noticed that she had a new pencil that looked just like mine.

I asked her, "Hey Ashley, where did you get that pencil?"

She said, "Don't worry about it because it is mine."

I said, "That's funny, I seem to have lost my pencil that looked just like it. Can I examine it closer?"

She said, "No, I don't have to let you see my pencil. Go away."

I said, "Well that's not very kind. I should inform you that I am going to tell Mrs. Walton, and I will be getting my pencil back."

Ashley said, "No chance. She will believe me before she believes you. Go ahead and tell her, tattletale."

I didn't let her know, but I could tell it was my pencil because I could see the letter "C" etched in the wood, near the top, by the metal, which held the eraser. I put the letter "C" on all of my pencils with the pointy end of my compass. It was so I could identify my pencil should they ever go missing.

Probably because of Ashley's name calling, I went directly up to Mrs. Walton and told her the story. She called Ashley up to her desk while I was standing there. Then she told her to go get the pencil in question.

She came back with the pencil and handed it to Mrs. Walton.

Mrs. Walton said, "Ashley, where did you get this pencil?"

Ashley said, ``I brought it from home. It's mine."

Mrs. Walton turned to me and said, "Do you have other pencils like this one?"

I said, "Yes, I will go and get one now."

When I got back, Ashley was standing with her arms crossed and had a mean look as she stared me down.

Handing her the pencil, I said, "Here you go Mrs. Walton."

Mrs. Walton took both pencils and held them up together. She matched up the "C's" which were on both pencils and showed them to Ashley.

Ashley's face turned white as a ghost as she stumbled on her words. "I, I, I, th, th, thought it was mine. Am I going to get in trouble?"

Mrs. Walton said, "No, Ashley I'm sure it was an honest mistake. Now head back to your seats."

As we walked back, I smiled at Ashley, and she gave me an even meaner look.

She then said, "Don't think that you are so cool because you got me in trouble. You will slip up, and I will get you back."

I said, "Hey, it's ok. I'm not upset. Like Mrs. Walton said, I'm sure it was an honest mistake. No worries."

Ashley huffed off and sat back in her seat.

Science class came around, and it seemed like Ashley was back to her old self. I made sure to stay away from her. My team was focused. We received our planning papers back so we could start our second round of planning and testing for the events.

For the model airplane, we were allowed to go outside near the windows where Mrs. Walton could still see us. Roosevelt and I went out while Eileen stayed in to work on the bridge design.

When we came back inside, Eileen said, "I have a design for the bridge that should hold a lot of weight. We are only allowed six pages of newspaper and glue to make our bridge. Here is my drawing of the bridge plan. If you like it, we should try to put it together now for a test run."

Eileen had each piece measured and labeled, so Roosevelt and I could help make the bridge. The rules stated that the bridge must be six inches high in the middle and at least fifteen inches long from end to end. Whichever teams' bridge held the most weight would win. We started following Eileen's directions and our bridge began to take shape. We had to wait for the glue to dry so our actual testing would have to be tomorrow.

I then showed Eileen and Roosevelt my plan for the egg drop.

I said, "Check this out. I brought in a metal lunch box filled with foam that was left over from my dad's foam bed he made for our Van. I even had an egg inside so we could test it. I thought we could stand on a chair, hold it high and drop it onto the grass. Unfortunately, it looks like we are out of time today. I will put it in my locker until tomorrow. We can test it then."

We came in the next day and our bridge was dry. I couldn't wait to see how much weight it would hold. If it falls down today, we would go back to the drawing board to come up with a new plan. I was also excited to check out our egg drop.

During science, we set little one-kilogram weights on our bridge. It held three of them which was a little over three pounds. We were skeptical about putting a fourth weight on because it seemed like it might collapse. We also thought that, if we had any chance to win the event, we would need to have the bridge hold more weight. Eileen placed the fourth kilogram weight on the bridge. It sagged in the middle and the legs gave way. We needed another plan. Eileen said she would draw up a new plan tonight.

I then went to my locker to get the lunch box so we could test to see if the egg would stay whole with a drop from eight feet. When I brought the lunch box into the classroom, I opened it and found the egg was cracked and the liquid inside was all over the foam. Someone had broken our egg between yesterday and today's class. I looked up from the lunch box at Ashley who was working with her group on their bridge. She looked right at me and quickly turned her head away. I couldn't prove it, but I would say she had something to do with our smashed egg.

I told Eileen and Roosevelt about the pencil incident. They agreed it could have been her who cracked the egg, but we had no proof.

I then said, "I will drop another egg inside the lunch box at home and let you know what happens."

At home, I held it up while standing on a chair. This was about eight feet from the ground. The box made a loud sound when it hit, and, when I opened it, the egg was cracked. I was so disappointed because I thought it would work. I really want to win this event or at least beat Ashley's team. I knew it would not survive a fall from a roof top that was fifteen feet high, so I came up with another plan. What came into my head was brilliant. My new plan would have to be kept top secret.

On the day of the class competition, our team was ready. Roosevelt had folded a paper airplane that was very streamline and looked like it could fly pretty far. We built the final bridge before we left school yesterday, and it looked stronger than the first bridge. I whispered my top-secret egg drop plan to my teammates.

I said, "I knew that the egg would crack if it was dropped from the roof, so I rigged a parachute around the lunch box to slow it down for a smooth landing."

Eileen asked, "Is that against the rules?"

I reminded her, "The rules that we were given said nothing about using a parachute. The only rule was the size of the box we were allowed to use which was twelve inches by twelve inches by twelve inches."

Eileen double checked the rule sheet and said, "I think you are right. A parachute rule does not exist. It could definitely help our egg land safely."

The first contest was the airplane flight for distance. All of the teams threw their planes one at a time. On our turn, Roosevelt stepped up to the start line. He threw it hard and within a few feet of the flight, it was hit by a downdraft and was headed to the ground early. Then, miraculously, it turned upward and sailed about ten feet further. It landed about a foot in front of everyone else's plane. We started jumping up and down and high fiving. Our plane was in first place!

Then Palo stepped up for Ashley's team and launched his plane into the air. It flew a similar path as our plane as it dove downward, curved upward and finally flew straight. It was coming down near where ours laid on the ground. We all moved forward to get a better look as it landed. From far away you couldn't tell, but, when we got closer, we could see that it was about an inch in front of our plane. Ashley, Palo and Sammy jumped up and down with an extra noisy celebration. After a few seconds, Palo respectively stopped his excitement. Ashley and Sammy looked at us and continued whooping it up. They were rubbing their victory in our faces. I definitely felt that they should be given a penalty for excessive celebration.

Roosevelt picked up our plane and we walked over to the egg drop location. Each team's entry or egg holder was in a paper shopping bag. Mr. Billy, our custodian, walked them up a ladder to the school roof. He then would drop one down and Mrs. Walton would go over to it when it landed. Before she would open the containers, she would announce the team's name that was on their box. Then she would open it and announce if the egg was intact, cracked or broken.

The first five that dropped were all in cardboard boxes and each one of them revealed a broken egg. The next egg was a team with a lunch box. It was not ours, but I was really curious to see if it would make it to the ground safely with the egg in one piece. When it hit the ground the lid, which was taped shut, came open and some of the contents of foam came out onto the ground. Mrs. Walton pulled out the egg, and it had many cracks in it but did not break.

Next, Mr. Billy pulled out a red rubber playground ball. I knew this had to be Ashley's team entry because it was the seventh drop and we both had not gone yet.

Roosevelt blurted out, "That's not a box, it's an illegal entry. The only rule was that your box should be no bigger than twelve inches, by twelve inches, by twelve inches."

Mrs. Walton didn't say anything, and Mr. Billy dropped the ball. It bounced about two feet off the ground before it rolled a little and laid to rest. I looked at it and saw that it was a rubber kickball that had a tear on the side. It must have been one of Mr. Howard's old one's that hadn't made the trash yet.

Mrs. Walton took the tape off of the tear on the ball and looked inside. She reached her hand in and pulled out some foam. Then she pulled out the egg. It did not have a crack in it at all. It survived the fall.

Some students in the crowd started yelling, "Cheater," "Rule breaker," and someone even said, "Anderson is disqualified."

Mr. Billy held up the last entry which was ours. It was a metal lunch box with a small parachute attached to it. My team was smiling.

Ashley saw the parachute and immediately said, "You're not allowed to use a parachute. That's illegal!"

I answered her back. "We just told you that the only rule was that your box needed to be no bigger than twelve inches by twelve inches by twelve inches, not a ball. We have a legal box. You didn't have a box. You need to follow the rules."

Mr. Billy dropped our lunch box from the roof.

At first the parachute did not unfold. I was holding my breath. Then, about half way down the chute opened up. The lunch box with the words, 'egg transit' on the side, began to float with grace down to the ground. It landed smoothly on the grass without even a bump.

Mrs. Walton opened up the lunchbox and pulled out the unscathed egg which had a smiley face drawn on it. The class began to chant, "Genius, genius, genius!"

I looked at Ashley and she had a frown and was shaking her head as if to say no. I had a big smile on my face and held my uncracked smiley face egg up in her direction. This act deserved a penalty too. She then ran up to Mrs. Walton and said, "That's unfair, they cannot use a parachute."

Mrs. Walton said to her, "Be careful Ashley. Your rubber ball was not a box and that is what the rules called for." Hearing those words, Ashley quieted down quickly.

We all headed inside as the bridge building contest was next.

Roosevelt wasn't done. He went closer to Ashley and said, "Cheater."

Ashley yelled back, "I am not. You are the cheater. I'm telling!"

She then went up to Mrs. Walton and said, "Roosevelt is calling me a cheater again. Everyone is calling me a cheater. It just isn't fair."

Mrs. Walton then spoke to the class, "Ok everyone, the Science Olympics will be canceled if we have anymore name calling."

The bridge building contest was exciting. Every bridge was collapsing after the first bridge held three kilograms. The rest of the groups had to put additional weight on their bridge if they wanted to win.

When Ashley put the four-kilogram weight on her bridge it collapsed like the others. Almost everyone cheered. Our bridge was next. Eileen carefully placed three of the one-kilogram weights next to each other near the center of our bridge. She had to put on another weight if we wanted to have any chance to win. She looked at me and Roosevelt. We both nodded to her as if to say, "Go ahead, put it on."

Eileen reached into her pocket and pulled out a half kilogram weight her dad gave her from his fishing tackle box. Our bridge did not collapse. Almost immediately, Ashley started yelling, "That's not fair. She is cheating! Nobody else has a half kilogram weight. If she has one, we all should have one."

The students in the room were calling out to Ashley now, "Poor sport", "Loser," and "Cry baby."

Ashley began to cry.

Mrs. Walton banged her wooden mallet on her wooden desk and announced in a disturbing sounding voice, "That's it! The contest is officially over. Have a seat!"

We all quietly went back to our seats.

After a few moments of silence, Mrs. Walton began to speak, "I want you all to know that we have to learn from our experiences. I know now that we need more detailed rules for our Science Olympics. I also believe the event was a good idea and that it will continue to be held each year for years to come. It is a great opportunity to get students more interested in science. You have to admit that making it a competition did spark some of your curiosities. However, because of a big oversight through unclear directions on my part, I apologize. At the same time, I believe that it's quite possible that unclear directions will be a part of future competitions. We should be forced to think outside of the box to achieve a better or newer way of doing things. If I had told you ahead of time that you could be as creative and imaginative as you wanted, we probably would not have had a problem with sportsmanship. That is something many of you must work on. Things are not always going to go your way, and, when they don't, you must learn from it and move on. Respecting your own dignity is something you should always strive for. If you can do that, it means that you are respecting the other competitors. None of you should let your emotions drive your responses to an extent where feelings are hurt. We have enough poor sports in our world. Please, from this point on, make it a point to remember to be a good sport in future competitions and in life. You are all good people. Let's keep it that way."

16 The Kickball Challenge

At the end of every school year there was the annual fifth grade kickball challenge. Mrs. Walton's class would take on Ms. Joseph's class. During the weeks leading up to this year's game, there was a lot of talk between classes as to who would win. Mr. Howard was going to run the game on the official softball field that was on the west side of the school. We never played there except on field day. A real lined softball field made this game seem extra special.

When Chucky asked Mr. Howard what the winners got, he said, "Bragging rights." His answer seemed kind of strange to me, as it was coming from a guy who constantly stressed good sportsmanship.

I thought our team would have an advantage in the game because we had more students who actually played kickball during recess than Ms. Joseph's class. The main rule was you had to have everyone in your class kick one time before switching sides. While in the field, you just kept trying to stop the other team from scoring runs. The number of outs didn't matter. Each team must also alternate kickers with a girl/boy order for as long as possible.

Ms. Joseph's class was first to kick while Mrs. Walton's class took the field. After their turn to kick, they had four runs. We switched sides, and our class was confident we would be ahead after this inning. To our surprise, we went through our line up and only scored three times. After that I figured it out, with twenty-four students in the field, it was going to be hard to score.

Ms. Joseph's class came up for the second time. This time Christopher Sanchez kicked a ball to right field and started running like he was going to go all the way for a home run. Eddie scooped it up in deep right field and threw it towards the infield. Christopher started to round third base and head for home. Big Palo, from our class, caught Eddie's ball near first base. He then turned and fired a hard and accurate throw toward home plate. The ball whizzed through the air like it was shot out of a cannon. Just before Christopher could reach home plate, the ball connected with the side of his head. It sounded like Mrs. Walton's wooden mallet crashing down on her desk. The power of the throw resulted in Christopher's body leaving the ground and going sideways into the air. When Christopher's hip hit the ground, his feet were above his head. He bounced and then rolled about eight feet away from home plate. In harmony, you could hear everyone from both teams' gasp, "Oh!"

Then you heard Andrew from our class yell, "You're out, Christopher!"

As soon as Christopher got up, he was as mad as a hornet that just got swatted out of the air. Mrs. Walton's team was high fiving in the field and congratulating Palo on such a great throw. Furious, Christopher started to run toward Palo who was near first base. Palo was double Christopher's size. He ran full speed at Palo who just stood there with a smile on his face. Before he reached Palo, I quickly ran over to head him off. Christopher ran into my outstretched left arm. I then grabbed his right side with my right hand. As I held him back, he begun to kick and swing his arms in the air just inches away from Palo's smiling face. Mr. Howard came over and pulled Christopher from my arms.

He then walked Christopher back to his team's bench and tried to calm him down.

Mr. Howard yelled, "Play on."

Ms. Joseph's class finished all of their turns and added two runs making their total score six.

Andrew announced, "You all have six runs, and we have three."

Then Ashley yelled out to everyone, "We have a no head shot rule, remember? If you get hit in the head you are safe. Christopher's run does count because he was hit in the head. The score is now seven for Ms. Joseph's class and we have three."

During our teams at bat, we were able to get four more runs, and the game was now tied seven to seven. Tia was on second base with Palo up to kick. He was our last and best kicker, so we were pretty confident about our chances to win. Palo kicked it into left field, and Susan Pervish caught it on one bounce. She threw it to Christopher, who then threw it at Tia as she was on her way to home plate. Tia was a talented athlete and must have sensed that the throw was coming. She looked over her shoulder, ducked while running, and the ball sailed over her head. For some reason the pitcher, James, who came in to take the throw at home plate wasn't quite ready. The ball bounced off his chest toward Tia who saw it and ducked a second time. She then touched home plate and Mrs. Walton's class won eight to seven.

After a short celebration, both teams lined up opposite one another and gave high fives. I noticed that Mr. Howard was near Christopher who was upset because they lost but did compose himself enough to give some high fives. I guess Mr. Howard taught us some sportsmanship after all.

17 Epic Sleepover (part 1)

In a very animated voice, Mrs. Walton announced, "Hear ye! hear ye! Calling all boys and girls. We are having our first ever fifth grade sleepover here at Washington Elementary. It will be held on a Saturday night. This will be a very memorable time. Please do not worry if you are not interested or your parents don't want you to come. It is certainly not a mandatory event. The night will only be held if we have at least fourteen students, and this includes Ms. Joseph's class. Please raise your hand if you think that you might come?"

I think every student had their mouths wide open and sat in shock while Mrs. Walton made her announcement. She also had Palo pass out a permission slip letter that explained everything.

I looked around and immediately could see that only two hands were not up. Since everyone was here today, that meant twenty-two students were into it.

There was a collective celebration of most everyone calling out, "Yes, yeah, yeah, yeah, woot, woot!" Mrs. Walton then slammed her hardback math book on the desk. There was silence. She could quiet a room in a variety of ways, but this moment definitely required a text book slam.

Mrs. Walton said, "Can we all control ourselves and let Tia read the permission slip so we can hear the details?"

Tia read, "On Saturday, May 20th,1978 we will be having a fifth-grade sleepover at Washington Elementary. The night will be filled with interesting games and activities. Each student must provide their own transportation to school and arrive by 6:30pm. Students should bring a pillow, sleeping bag, toothbrush, toothpaste, and a towel. Pajamas are also encouraged, but you can sleep in sweat pants or shorts if you prefer. Parents must pick up students on Sunday morning, May 21st at 9:00am sharp. Please sign the bottom of this page and have your child return the form to their teacher on or before Wednesday, May 17th. If you wish to chaperone, please check the box below. Chaperones will be selected from a hat as we only need six total. Sincerely, your fifth grade teachers."

The excitement was so big I was about to bust! Luckily, it was the end of the school day, and we were getting ready to walk home. As we walked out of the room, I felt like I was on a cloud. Other fifth graders were high fiving and smiling ear to ear. My buddy James came out of Ms. Joseph's class and practically tackled me. He threw his body up into mine, and I wasn't quite ready so I ended up banging against the lockers. It didn't matter. We were totally psyched.

"This night is going to be epic," said James. We then started our walk toward the front of the school.

"You got that right buddy. I can't wait to find out what games and activities they have planned for us," I then asked, "How many kids in your class were interested."

James said, "Almost all of them."

I said, "That's good. We had all but two kids who showed an interest. That's at least forty kids who could possibly come. They might have to add a few more chaperones."

As the deadline to hand in your permission form approached, we only had ten students committed so far. We were all hopeful that the other parents were waiting until the exact due date.

We hoped that they were holding the permission slip as bribery for good behavior.

On Wednesday the 17th, Mrs. Walton reported that she had fourteen permission slips from our class. That was enough to have the night even without Ms. Joseph's class. It turns out that they had ten kids who turned in forms.

The day before our Saturday night school event we were told to come through the main doors and make our way to the gym with all of our sleepover gear. Parents should sign in their student and exit immediately unless they were going to be chaperones.

I was one of the first to arrive for this exciting night at 6:15pm. My mom walked with me to the gym, signed me in, gave me a hug, and said, "Have fun. See you in the morning."

The sun was still out, but you could tell it was getting late as the sun was now shining through the back of the school which I had never seen before. In the gym I found Eileen Dottson, Sammy Smith and, to my surprise, the quiet girl Hellen Matters. There were two chaperones standing with them and my goodness Hellen's mom looked just like her! The other man had to be Sammy's dad as he was kind of short, just like Sammy.

We were told where to put our stuff down and that we could play with some of the gym equipment that Mr. Howard had left out for us. I shot some hoops with Sammy while Eileen and Hellen did some hula hooping. I couldn't believe Hellen had jelly shoes on and sweatpants. I don't think anyone ever saw her wear anything other than colorful sun dresses and shiny black dress shoes.

More kids, teachers, and chaperones walked into the gym. It was a steady stream of people for about five minutes. When it seemed like all the students were present, Mrs. Walton took out a megaphone and welcomed everyone. We all sat down in the middle of the gym for further instructions about the night's events.

She announced, "We will be starting out with a partner scavenger hunt. You will attempt to find eight items that are located throughout the school and bring them back to the gym. You are allowed to run, and you can look inside any door that is open. You may not go into desks or move any furniture. The only things you can touch are the items you are collecting, your feet on the floor, and your partner if necessary. Chaperones will be strategically watching and disqualifying teams who break any rules. There is also a time limit. In eighteen minutes, you will hear me on the loudspeaker giving you a two-minute warning that you need to be back inside the gym. If you do not get back in twenty minutes time, your team will be disqualified from the competition. Just so you know the main lights throughout the school must remain off. The school district wants us to conserve electricity. The only lighting will come from one emergency light per room and within each hallway."

There were twelve teams with two students on each one. Thankfully, Andrew was assigned to be my partner. He was fast, competitive and we even had matching high-top sneakers.

We were told that the items on the list were everyday school items but that they might not be easy to find due to limited lighting. Each team was given an envelope which contained the list of items to search for.

Mrs. Walton announced, "You may open your envelope on the start signal. She held everyone's attention in the palm of her hand. You could hear a pin drop.

Then, without a real warning, she blew the whistle and everyone tore into their envelopes. For a moment, it was like seagulls flapping while tearing into a slice of pizza. One second later, teams started running.

The list included:

five-line chalk holder

metal lunchbox

foam ball

metric tape measure

ditto paper sheet

calculator

cassette tape

one piece of cursive writing paper

Andrew and I were just running down the gym hallway toward the front of the school without a plan. Running at full speed in the hallway while at school felt great. I think I was running faster than I ever have in my entire life. Suddenly, I decided to stop.

I grabbed Andrew's arm and said, "Wait, let's just go into a classroom and get what we can. Then we should keep going to other classrooms until we find everything."

As we stood there, three groups whizzed right by us headed for the upper grade level classrooms.

We started running again, but I stopped Andrew a second time and said, "Hey what's the hardest item to find on the list?"

Andrew glanced at the list and said, "Maybe the lunchbox because most kids bring theirs home?"

"Exactly," I said.

"Let's check the lost and found. It's right here by the front door. Look, a bright pink metal mermaid lunch box! At least four groups must have run right by it. Oh yeah, and it's the only one! What's next?"

Andrew said, "Everything else looks like it would be in a fourth or fifth grade classroom except the foam ball."

I said, "I think we can get the foam ball back in Mr. Howard's gym closet. Let's get that at the end."

We started sprinting toward the upper grade classrooms. I knew we needed to find our own empty classroom. We passed third and fourth grade rooms that were all occupied.

"Come on," I said. "Let's go to our room."

Nobody was there, but we were now the farthest team away from the gym. We had to work fast.

"I got the five-line chalk holder and the metric tape!" said Andrew. Both were on the chalkboard tray.

I said, "I got the calculator from Mrs. Walton's desk. And here is a piece of cursive writing paper! We just need the ditto sheet, a cassette tape, and a foam ball."

I continued, "Follow your nose for the ditto sheet. Let's go to the teacher's room where they have a mimeograph machine. I know they have the machine in that room because it smells like potent ink every time we walk by there."

"What about the cassette tape?" asked Andrew.

"There must be one in the music room, and it's on our way."

We ran to the music room and there were kids coming out of it. My heart skipped a beat. Were we too late? As we went inside, we looked around on the shelves.

"There they are in the box marked cassettes," said Andrew.

"We cannot reach them," I said.

"Just stand on a chair," said Andrew.

"No," I said. "If a chaperone sees us move a chair we will be disqualified. Give me a boost."

Andrew clasped his hands together and I placed my foot in them. I counted to three and up I went. I reached over the side of the already open box. There must have been a hundred cassettes in there. I grabbed one, and Andrew let me down.

As I came down, a chaperone was staring right at us and said, "Good job not using the chair. One group was already disqualified."

We then ran out of the room and sprinted toward the teachers' room. The hallway was darker now. The sun had completely set and the hall lights were dim, but you could still see fairly well. As we approached the door, the smell of ditto ink was quite potent.

"Grab a ditto out of the trash," I said.

Andrew reached down and pulled out a ditto paper. His hand turned a dark shade of purple from the ink smear that was on the paper. As he held up the wet paper he said, "This one must have been a recent mistake. It's definitely a ditto paper."

"Let's book it to the gym," I said. Before my words finished, Andrew was already running out of the room.

"Wait. Let's put some of this stuff in the lunchbox so we don't drop it," I said. We then put the calculator, cursive writing sheet, ditto sheet, metric measuring tape, and cassette tape in the lunchbox and closed it tight. Andrew held the five-line chalk holder in his hand.

I held the lunchbox like it was a football under my arm as we sprinted down the hall to the gym. We went right past some teachers and chaperones to Mr. Howards equipment closet which was wide open. Unfortunately, there was no emergency light. As soon as we entered the closet the loudspeaker gave a horn sound followed by Mrs. Walton's announcement, "All teams must report to the gym in two minutes or be disqualified."

The pressure was on us with no foam ball, and we were running out of time. I reminded Andrew not to move anything. Just after I said that, a chaperone appeared in the doorway. It's like they had some sort of mental telepathy and knew when to watch for cheating. Mr. Howard had a lot of items on shelves and in buckets, barrels and boxes. It was dark and nothing was labeled, so we were struggling to see what was in some of the containers.

Andrew said, "Let's go back with seven items. At least we won't get disqualified."

"No," I said with determination, "Some teams might have eight items, and we won't win. Let's keep looking." We looked some more but could not find a foam ball. The loud speaker came on again.

This time Mrs. Walton said, "Thirty seconds."

I looked at Andrew and he at me. He shook his head and inched back toward the closet entrance. The chaperone was intensely watching us, as if we were about to make a mistake.

I said, "Come on Andrew, eyes wide open. It's got to be here. Plus, we are already in the gym."

Andrew was pulling on my arm and said, "Technically, we are in a closet, not the gym. Let's go."

Andrew was in the gym and I was still in the closet. He pulled my arm, and I pulled back. Either I kind of gave in or he pulled harder, but I was now standing in the gym with him.

I said, "Hold on I think I saw something round in the corner as you pulled me out." I went back inside.

Andrew said, "Come on, the horn is about to sound."

I looked down at the floor in the corner and there it was. Surrounded by dust, hair, and fuzz was an old foam ball looking right at me. I yelled to Andrew, "I got it!"

I reached down, scooped it up with the dust, hair, and fuzz still attached. Then we hurried to the middle of the gym where teams were gathering.

Each team was standing behind a hula hoop in the order that they came into the gym. All teams were holding their scavenger hunt findings. We were standing by the fourth hoop. I looked to my left at the top three finishers, and only one other team had a metal lunch box.

Two more teams entered the gym just in time. There were two teams sitting against the gym wall. They looked sad, as they were apparently disqualified for moving furniture during the game. Six teams were now lined up.

The odd horn sounded, and Mrs. Walton came on the loudspeaker and said, "Sorry, but any team that is not in the gym is now disqualified."

Four teams didn't make it back in time. Two of them came in right after the horn sounded and were directed to sit against the wall by the disqualified teams. They were not happy as they walked toward the other disgruntled teams. About thirty seconds later the last two teams arrived and were directed to sit with the other disappointed kids.

Ms. Joseph announced through the megaphone, "All six teams by the hula hoops should now place their scavenger hunt items within their hoop."

I was so proud at this moment because I knew we had all eight items even though we were standing and showing just the lunchbox, the five-line chalk holder, and a dusty foam ball.

I quickly looked to our left at the three teams who were in the gym before us, and it was the team of Tia and Ashley who had the only other lunch box. Oh, how I wanted to win this game against them! They unloaded their lunchbox and I did the same. I could see all of their items and they were missing a foam ball.

I hit Andrew on the arm and whispered, "I think we won. They don't have a foam ball."

Mrs. Walton went down the line and announced the number of each team's items. The gym was silent and dark. With no light coming in the windows, it felt as if we were all in a large cave with minimal light. Squinting to see, we all focused on Mrs. Walton.

She announced, "Lenny Dale and Palo Regal, seven items. Susan Pervish and Eileen Dottson, seven items. Ashley Anderson and Tia

Rainey, seven items. Andrew Schmidt and Calvin Arthur, eight items. Ladies and gentlemen, we have our first ever fifth grade sleepover scavenger hunt winners!"

Andrew and I started jumping up and down and giving each other high tens. We were so happy to pull off the first ever night school scavenger hunt victory. Not only did we win two mini blueberry pies, our names would be going on the new *Wall of Fame Scavenger Hunt Champions* sign which would be located in the gymnasium. All the kids mingled around and talked about how much fun they had and how, or where, they found their items.

We all sat down for snack time. Everyone was given pretzels, potato chips, candy and chocolate milk. Andrew and I proudly ate our blueberry pies. Ashley had a miserable look on her face. She looked at me, and I smiled back at her with a little extra blueberry around my lips.

As we finished up our snack, Mr. Howard announced, "For our next challenge you will all be separated into two teams for a game of Capture the Bears!"

18 Epic Sleepover (part 2)

As we all stood huddled together in the middle of the poorly lit and dreary looking gym, all eyes were on Mr. Howard. You could feel the excitement in the air.

Mr. Howard continued, "The two teams will be named the Creamsicles and the Sorbets. In order to make the student numbers on each team even, the Creamsicles, will be made up of all of Ms. Joseph's students plus Andrew and Calvin. The 'Sorbets' will be the rest of Mrs. Walton's class. The Capture the Bears game is similar to the game we all know as Capture the Flag. There are seven stuffed bears hidden throughout the school. When a player finds a bear, it is theirs. Nobody can take a bear out of anyone's hand. A player who finds a bear should take it directly to the main office and give it to Mrs. Walton who will keep score. She will announce each score over the loud speaker. Once again, nobody can move any object in the school except a bear. Chaperones will be watching."

Mr. Howard then added, "You have two minutes to talk with your team and come up with a plan. Oh yeah, each player on the winning team will get ice cream, a cookie, and bragging rights. The losing team gets one cookie per player. The game will last for a maximum of forty minutes. The team with the most bears will be declared the winner. Your two minutes of planning begin now."

Both groups quickly formed their own huddle. A few people started talking at the same time on our team. It was hard to focus on what anybody was saying. I didn't hear a plan that made a lot of sense. Then I decided to take charge. I spoke up and said, "Stop talking, I have a plan!" The intensity in the sound of my voice was real. The team all stepped closer to listen.

I continued, "There are sixteen classrooms: four kindergarten rooms downstairs with twelve first through fifth grade classrooms upstairs. Plus, we have the library, music room, art room, cafeteria and two teacher rooms. There are only twelve of us. Everyone should start in a separate classroom and look thoroughly in it for at least five to ten minutes. James and Eileen should look in the fourth and fifth grade rooms. Andrew and I will take the four kindergarten rooms. If you find a bear, run and turn it in. Then go help look in a different room or go to a special area room. Remember do not change rooms until you've made a thorough search. If you find one tell…"

"Honk, honk, honk." The sound system really sounded like it was a goose on its last leg. Mrs. Walton announced, "You may now begin."

The two gym doors swung open, and both teams ran out in a double line formation at top speed. We made the turn to go down the surfing hill hallway, and I heard someone go down behind me. "Woooo, uugh!." I glanced back. It was Christopher from our team who crashed into Tia which meant one student from each team went down. Everyone else kept running. Students from each team peeled off to run down the two different classroom hallways. Andrew and I went towards the stairwell to head downstairs to the kindergarten classes. We were joined by Eddie and Sammy of the Sorbets team.

As we ran to the bottom of the steps, Eddie said, "Don't be traitor's guys and help us find the bears. We will give you some ice cream when we win."

Andrew said, "No chance buddy. We can't trust you."

Andrew went into room number one, and I ran to room number two. Eddie followed me in, and I wasn't sure where Sammy went. When I looked inside, I stopped cold in my tracks. There was a wall of at least seventy stuffed animals. I stared for a minute and scanned the large group. It was dark so I tried squinting, but I still could not see a bear. I thought maybe it was a trick. Maybe there wasn't a bear in the mountain of stuffed animals at all. I scanned some more. Eddie was standing next to me scanning too. Because the lighting was so dim, staring at all of those colors, shapes, sizes and different animals was starting to get painful. I looked away for a second to clear my head. Eddie was still scanning, and I started up again. At this point, the loudspeaker came on.

"Ashley Anderson scores one point for the Sorbets." I couldn't believe how fast she scored. I immediately wondered where she found the bear. Hopefully, someone saw her, and they know not to waste time looking in that room.

I looked away again from the huge pile of stuffed animals and scanned the room. I saw a stuffed animal sitting in the far corner of the room. I wanted to get it immediately, but desks and Eddie were in my way. I stepped forward as if I saw one in the big pile in front of us. Eddie stepped forward and, at that moment, I ran behind him to the far corner and scooped up a stuffed bear.

"Yes, I got one! See ya, Eddie."

I took off out of the room and yelled to Andrew, "I got a bear, I'll be back."

When I ran up the steps and into the main hallway, it was really dark. Only a small dim light hung from the ceiling. It was dark throughout the school so I couldn't run my fastest. I didn't want to crash into someone and lose the bear. I made it to the office and proudly handed my bear to Mrs. Walton.

Over the loudspeaker she announced, "Calvin Arthur scores one point for the Creamsicles! The score is now one to one. Keep looking everyone. Five bears to go."

I went back down to the kindergarten area as I knew there were at least two more classrooms that we had to check. I ran into Andrew in the dimly lit hallway. He said, "No bear in room number one, so I'm going to look in room three. Why don't you check room number four?"

I went into room number four, and Eddie was already in there looking. In his unwelcoming voice, he said, "If it isn't the toad boy again."

I responded, "Eddie, you do realize how small you are and how you will need me on your side in Middle School? If nobody likes you here, then how will they like you in sixth grade? Just a suggestion, but you might try being kind."

I scanned the dark room and didn't see anything, but the toy corner certainly drew my eye's attention. Then I saw it. A bear sitting up on a bookshelf looking right at me. Eddie saw it at the same time. We both started over towards it. When we got about six feet away, Eddie illegally slid a chair in front of me to slow me down. He then jumped up and knocked the bear off of the shelf. Eddie fell and the bear was laying on the ground between us. Just then a chaperone looked in the room and yelled, "Hey, I heard furniture move in here and that's against the rules." My shins were still touching the chair, and I was bent over it with one hand on the floor. It looked like I had moved it. Eddie picked up the bear and said, "I didn't move a chair. It was him." Then he ran out of the room. I told the chaperone that Eddie slid the chair into me.

The chaperone, who I think was Sammy's father said, "Well I didn't see it, so it's your word against his. Play on."

I ran to room three where Andrew and Sammy were walking around inspecting every detail. I called Andrew over and said, "Come on, let's go up to another room. Odds are that they didn't hide more than two bears in the kindergarten rooms. Eddie just got number two down here."

We ran out leaving Sammy by himself. Andrew and I ran up the moonlit steps. We ran down the dark hallway headed for the music room. As soon as we arrived, the loudspeaker came on again. Mrs. Walton said, "Eddie Monroe scores bear number three. It's two points for the Sorbets and one point for the Creamsicles."

Andrew and I ran to the music room and found Ava Johansson from the Sorbet team. In her deep Swedish voice, she said, "Hello my friendly foes."

I thought that was weird, but I said, "Hello Ava."

The music room was really dark as it only had one dim emergency light on. We walked around and scanned the room but initially didn't see anything. Once again, the loudspeaker came on.

Mrs. Walton announced, "Hellen Matters scores a bear for the Creamsicles. It's now a tie game with the Sorbets two and the Creamsicles two. Three bears remain."

Andrew said to me, "That's amazing that Hellen found a bear."

I said, "I know, but I'm not surprised, as she does have a keen sense about her."

Andrew and I were now squinting as we examined the music room shelves. They were deep shelves so it really made it hard to see everything on each shelf.

Then Ava said, "Oh boys, is this what you are looking for?"

She held up a stuffed bear and started doing a celebration dance. I said, "Uugh, how'd you find that bear in this dark dungeon?"

She said, "It found me. I tripped over it, as it was sticking out from under the bottom of the risers."

She ran out and said, "Bye boys."

Andrew and I immediately knew we needed to look in another room. I said, "Let's check the teachers' room."

We went out into the hallway and were almost run over by James.

He kept running and said, "I got one!"

"Nice," I said. "I think there is one bear left, and it's a tie score."

Mrs. Walton announced, "Ava Johansson scores! It's now three bears for the Sorbets and two bears for the Creamsicles. Two bears to go. Wait a minute. James Hopper scores for the Creamsicles! It's all tied up with only one bear to go!"

Before we entered the teachers' room, we ran into Eileen Dottson. She said, "Hold on you guys. I have a hunch. The names of our teams are the Creamsicles and the Sorbets. I believe the last bear might be in the cafeteria kitchen, possibly near the ice cream cooler."

Before she said anything else, I said, "Let's go."

We hightailed it down the hallway which went slightly downhill to the cafeteria. We were practically flying as I felt the wind going past my ears. There were a few kids in there looking under the cafeteria tables.

Eileen whispered, "Let's go in the back and check the ice cream coolers."

When we arrived, the coolers were locked and there was no bear in sight. As we stood there, we began hearing voices in the very back part of the kitchen area. We moved toward them, and we could see four outlines of humans gathered around a dumb waiter shaft. The dumb waiter connected to the outside and was used for food, milk and ice cream deliveries.

We walked toward the back and the silhouettes were now recognizable. It was Sammy, definitely his dad, Palo, and Ava who was one step ahead of us again. Andrew, Eileen and myself were on the opposite team, and we were unfortunately too late.

Sammy said, "I found it first so it's mine."

I said, "What are you talking about? It's not in your hand, so it's not yours."

We all looked down the open shaft of the dumb waiter and could see the bear lying on what was actually the top of the dumb waiter.

"Why would anyone hide the bear down there?" I asked.

Ava said, "When I arrived, the bear was stuck between the ropes as if it were hanging on." I saw Sammy reach for it and then watched it fall."

"I did not make it fall. It fell by itself," Sammy replied.

This was beginning to look fishy, as I thought to myself why was Sammy's dad near Sammy again? He knows where the bears are, and he probably wants Sammy to get one so he can get his name announced and also win the game.

Eileen said, "Because we don't have the starting key, we cannot move the dumb waiter. That means our only chance to get the bear is to lower Ava down to get it."

Andrew said, "Eileen, Ava is on the other team. I can go down."

Eileen said, "You could go down, but, no offense, you do weigh a lot and we would have a hard time pulling you out. We need you, Calvin and Palo to pull Ava out."

Sammy said, "I found it. I'm going to go down."

Eileen was a quick thinker, and she was quite direct. She said, "The words on the side of the wall say *eight feet nine-inch shaft height*. You would not be tall enough for us to reach you and pull you back up. Ava is the only one who can do it. Remember she is six feet tall. Your team will still win, but, even though Andrew and Calvin are on the other team, they have to be willing to help pull her out. Palo won't be able to do it on his own."

Sammy was still pouting. "I found it. It should be mine."

I couldn't resist with his dad standing there. I said, "You are in fifth grade Sammy, and still selfish. Newsflash, your team is still going to win."

Eileen said, "You can let Ava get it, or we can leave it and both teams will end in a tie.

According to my watch, we have two minutes left before the game is declared over."

"OK," said Sammy with a shadowy disgruntled look on his face and his arms crossed.

Ava turned around on her belly and put her legs down into the shaft. There was a bar at the top that she could hang from. With her height and arm length she was really close to the top of the dumb waiter. She hung there for a few seconds.

With panic in her voice she pleaded, "I don't want to jump. Please help me!"

Andrew said, "My shoulder is hurting from football. Calvin, you and Palo can do it."

Palo and I laid down and each grabbed one of her wrists.

I said, "We have you. Let go of the bar and we will lower you the rest of the way."

Ava said, "Ok, please be careful."

She let go, and we lowered her down about two inches so she could stand.

Ava said, "That was easy. I got the bear. Now please pull me out of this dark hole."

Sammy said, "Throw the bear up. It will be easier."

Ava said, "I already stuffed it in my shirt."

Palo and I reached down and grabbed Ava's wrists to pull her up. Once she got a hold of the bar, she used her feet to walk up the wall while we grabbed her under her arms. One tug and she came right out. Just then the announcements came on. Mrs. Walton said, "All participants make their way back to the gymnasium. You have one minute until the game ends."

With that, we all started running back through the cafeteria and up the small hill hallway toward the office. Before we got to the office entrance, Ava stopped, grabbed my arm and said, "Calvin, I want you and I to hold the bear when we turn it in. Please grab one of the bear's paws, and we will turn it in together. After all, we couldn't have gotten it without you."

Sammy said, "No, that bear is ours. You can't share it."

I answered back, "Shame on you Sammy. What would your dad (who was standing a few feet away) say about being a good sport? It's just a game Sammy."

Palo stepped in front of Sammy just in case he tried something. Palo understood sportsmanship. Ava held out the bear towards me, and I grabbed a paw. Then we ran the rest of the way to the main office where Mrs. Walton gave her announcements. As she saw us coming toward her, Mrs. Walton's big eyes grew bigger. She looked at her stopwatch and spoke into the microphone in front of her. "Unbelievable folks, we have the last bear. Ava Johansson of the Sorbets and Calvin Arthur of the Creamsicles have turned in the bear together. Both teams have split the last point. The Capture the Bear game ends in an historic tie!"

19 The End or Beginning

In our homeroom on the last day of school, I said to Brandon, "It's hard to believe that in less than an hour we will be graduating fifth grade."

He said, "Yeah and what's even more weird is we might not ever come back to this school again."

"Holy cow," I replied. "We have a lot of memories from this old building!"

As we cleaned up the remains of Mrs. Walton's wall art, posters, and center activities, I felt a bit somber.

I went up to Mrs. Walton and said, "I want to thank you before the assembly and the end of school for all that you did for me and our class. We will never forget our time here."

Mrs. Walton said, "You and your classmates will always be in my thoughts. Good luck to you Calvin. I expect to hear big things from you."

We then all got in line to go to the gym for our graduation ceremony. I stood there feeling heavy-hearted as I knew we were now at the end of our Wash El time.

I whispered to Brandon, "This might be our last walk in a line because, in sixth grade, we don't walk as a class anywhere."

Brandon said, "Yeah, there are a lot of last and first things happening for us today. Isn't it exciting?"

I said, "Yeah, I guess it's time to say good bye and face the reality that we are going to a new school for sixth grade."

It was unfortunate that Tia, Ashley, Roosevelt, Lenny, and Eileen were all absent today with the chickenpox. There were also six kids absent from Ms. Joseph's class. It felt strange not having all of the students present on such a big day.

Mrs. Walton chose me to be the graduation speaker. It made me feel very proud. I also felt very nervous as I would be speaking in front of parents, grandparents and my remaining classmates.

I summoned up my courage, and stood proudly on the stage looking over the crowd of spectators. I touched the microphone to see if it was on and then read my speech.

"I must say our time at Washington Elementary was full of valuable experiences. We learned many lessons from our teachers, and from each other. In my mind, our special events were also a big part of our learning, and I hope we will all remember them forever. I will highlight those I thought were special to me and possibly to each one of you. We always had scary fun every year on Halloween. We bonded at lunch time, especially the day Chucky ate the inedible lunch in fourth grade. We always looked forward to recess, field days and field trips. Going back to colonial times was really awesome. We helped to build each other's character through partner activities, team sports on recess, cooperation in PE class, and completing group projects in science. We also learned about our emotions through teasing, being humiliated, and a lot of jealous situations. Who could forget the time we grew up in "The Talk" lesson. Most of us were poor sports in the Science Olympics. We failed that test, but we learned what not to act like in the future. After failing, we bounced back. With our dignity in check, we learned how to be disappointed and how to laugh at ourselves. It took a while, but in the end, I felt like we did learn to respect our differences. I wouldn't be thorough if I didn't mention the intensity and perseverance we learned through kickball, spelling tests, state tests, and that very special epic sleepover event we all loved! Yes, my friends, we are leaving here and going on different pathways to our future, but we'll always have Wash El in common. I want to thank each and every one of the students for contributing to our great experiences. I also especially want to thank our teachers who dedicated their lives to us when we needed them the most. If we don't come back to visit Wash El, please know that you will always be in our thoughts. Although this is the end, it really is also a beginning. I'm sure sixth grade will be full of fun and challenging adventures. After all of our experiences here, we are definitely ready and up for anything sixth grade has to offer. Good luck everyone. Be safe. Be strong and have fun. We are outta here!"

At that moment everyone stood and cheered. I smiled ear to ear. The applause seemed to last for about two minutes, but it was probably more like twenty seconds. Mrs. Walton then walked over and gave me an awkward hug that I wasn't expecting.

She then took my spot by the microphone and said, "Thank you Calvin and thank you 'new' sixth graders. Please sign out with your parents at the table or head back to your classroom one more time."

I made my way through the crowd, gave some high tens and found my mom. She also gave me a big hug. Then she asked, "Do you want to stay here at school or go home with me?"

I looked down at the new itchy red dots on my arm and said, "I think it's time to go home."

Final Comment

Calvin Arthur just finished a fifth grade year full of opportunities to improve himself. His quest for courage was slow at the beginning, but then grew and became stronger as the school year progressed. Calvin's final year at Washington Elementary School had its challenges, and Calvin took many of them head on.

Mrs. Walton was above and beyond the best teacher to bring out Calvin's ultimate character. She gave him great opportunities to develop confidence and grow as a class influencer. Many of the students also played a big part in developing Calvin's leadership, decision making and determined personality. All of this occurred at a time when many students did not show empathy for others. In the beginning, like many kids, he remained quiet. There were also times when Calvin was knocked down a few rungs on the imaginary classroom social ladder. On one day, he was the target for three bullies and the pain they inflicted was very uncomfortable. This was the year he figured out that he was in his own way when he encountered stressful situations. He began to recognize his emotional low points and realized these times actually gave him the push he needed to gain more confidence. Towards the end, courage was found, as Calvin took charge and stood up for what was right. He had become more confident, strong minded, and actually enjoyed the challenges his teachers and classmates provided.

His earned leadership and classmate respect will ultimately be tested at his new school in sixth grade. Will he return to his introverted self or stay vocal and make good choices? Will Calvin give in to Middle School peer pressure and get into trouble? Stay tuned for another formidable school year in the third book of the Calvin Arthur series, *"On Calvin Arthur's 6th Grade Cross Roads ~ Internal Struggle."*

Please, if you have read this far, can you go back and leave a comment on Amazon? It will definitely help to keep the book's messages alive for others. Thank you, R.A. Stone.

About the Author

R. A. Stone is an award winning thirty-two-year veteran elementary and middle school teacher. His career in teaching took place within six different public schools. The Calvin Arthur series was inspired by his daily observations and interactions with students over so many years in education.

His passions have been storytelling and writing since his early elementary school days. R.A. recognized then and throughout his career that the student held emotional curriculum in schools was and is very real. We can all learn from what Calvin and his classmates experienced.

Special Note

If you or someone you know has been a victim to a bully go directly to a trusted adult. If they do not help, you should go to another trusted adult. It's hard to put it all in perspective but remember the bully needs your help. Be courageous and speak up. For more information on bullying and how to get help now visit stopbullying.gov.